Seducing Dionysus

Come Sail Away!

[illegible]

Modern Mythica Book 2

Seducing Dionysus

Aria Skylar

4 Horsemen
Publications, Inc.

4 Horsemen
Publications, Inc.

4 Horsemen Publications, Inc.
1497 Main St. Suite 169
Dunedin, FL 34698
4horsemenpublications.com
info@4horsemenpublications.com

Cover & Typesetting by Niki Tantillo
Edited by Jen Paquette

Library of Congress Control Number: 2023930775

Paperback ISBN-13: 978-1-64450-826-8
Audiobook ISBN-13: 978-1-64450-827-5
Ebook ISBN-13: 978-1-64450-828-2

To my husband, who is always there for me.

Table of Contents

"Lovers don't finally meet somewhere.
They're in each other all along."

— Rumi

At last. Thomas was hers.

Arynne watched him stand there on the balcony of their hotel room, the tropical sun setting, silhouetting his form. The wind pulled at his light clothes and dark hair, making him seem like the romantic hero from a novel.

She walked up behind him and slipped her arms around his middle, tracing her fingers over his well-sculpted muscles to squeeze him tightly. Possessively.

"We did it," she whispered into his neck, the highest her lips could reach, before laying a kiss against her whisper. His larger hand encircled her joined ones, holding them fast against him.

"This is like a dream," he said softly. She felt the rumble of his voice reverberate through her.

"But it's real," she answered, smiling. "We're finally together and nothing can tear us apart now."

"You shouldn't say that."

She chuckled. "You mean I'm tempting Fate? Should I knock on some wood or something?" she quipped.

He turned in her arms and cupped her face with his hands, looking deeply into her eyes. His normally blue ones were black in the dying light, like twin pools of a hungry abyss.

She didn't wait for him to act, pressing herself and her lips to his and drinking him in. His tongue was reluctant at first, like it had been every time they kissed, as if he were afraid to enter the sacred place that was her mouth. But she invited him in, coaxed him until he yielded into her beautifully and made her insides sing with divine music.

This was meant to be.

He was meant to be hers.

His hands roved over her body, pulling at the sundress she wore, as if trying to find a way through the fabric so he could tear it away. She actually liked that dress, white with blue flowers, so she removed it herself. Slipping the spaghetti straps off her shoulders, she wiggled so the material yielded over her generously curvy form to pool at her feet. Normally, her large chest would have been contained within a bra, but she had chosen to not wear one for him, and his gaze on her bare skin now made the flaunting of societal pressures worth it.

His hands slipped over the newly revealed curves of her bosom, pinching at the soft pinks of her nipples before enveloping one with his mouth. Her face twisted into desperate savor as her lover sucked, sending jolts of electricity to her toes and back up to her core. She arched back against him, and his arms came around to support her.

Yet they were so off-balance as he devoured her that eventually they both yielded to gravity and landed on the bed. Quickly, the rest of her sundress was pulled down and discarded, along with the slip of underwear she had been wearing. He knelt on the ground before her and threw both of her legs over his shoulders, cupping her butt with his hands to bring her to him. She cried out in sensual abandon, heedless of the opinions of neighbors or the hotel staff. She needed this, this full-throated declaration of her true self after months, and frankly years, of suppression in her father's house. It only urged her Thomas on, and he sought out every cranny of her body, eliciting ecstatic energies before laying a kiss on her inner thigh.

She felt breathless and desired as their eyes met. She lay vulnerable before him, naked while he was still clothed. She wanted him like her. She wanted to feel his skin on hers, but before she could move to make her desire a reality, he undid the fly of his khaki pants. Slipping his member out, he leaned in, brushing the tip against her own bud of pleasure, slick from his ministrations. She groaned again, burning to feel him inside her.

"I never asked," he said suddenly. "Are you a virgin?"

"No," she breathed, a pang of fear stabbing through her. Was that something he had been expecting? They had never talked about it. They really hadn't known each other that long, but the passion flaming within wouldn't allow them to deny their feelings, even if they were hasty.

But now? When everything was over, and they had successfully escaped her father's control, there was time to ask such questions.

"Does that matter?" she whispered softly, tremulous at the answer.

"No," he assured softly and leaned in to kiss her delicately on the lips. "I just didn't want to hurt you."

Then he pressed himself in. Her breath caught, not from pain but the overwhelming sensation of him filling her. She had not lied—she was not a virgin—but neither did she have much experience. He rocked within her, and the zipper from his pants bit into her thigh. Yet it did nothing to deter the sensations coursing through her. In fact, it was incredibly sexy, her naked while he was fully clothed and powerful. He cupped her head again, this time with his elbows on the bed, and she felt his speed increase.

Except it wasn't going anywhere. She loved it, but she felt like she was climbing a mountain and not quite reaching its peak. She couldn't figure out why. Thomas seemed to be climbing without her, going higher and higher while she remained stuck at the midway point. She thought with him it would be different. This time she would feel that deep satisfaction her other two one-time lovers had found from this act. She could feel it was possible; she could feel her whole being want it. Yet, just like before, it didn't come. It didn't just happen.

What was wrong with her?

And then his body shuddered. He groaned and arched his back, spasming against her.

Into her.

After a few heartbeats, it was over. He collapsed, breathing heavily, and she was left as she had been before—alone and unfulfilled.

They remained that way for a few moments longer, him catching his breath and her filling with doubts.

"Are you alright?" he asked, finally lifting up to look down into her face. His care and concern warmed her, easing the doubts away. "Did you cum?"

She looked away, unable to meet his eyes. Stabs of shame pierced through her at her failure to do what should have come naturally. His fingers pinched at her chin and turned her back.

"No," she admitted and pressed her hands against her face, to hide the burning in her cheeks.

He kissed the backs of her knuckles. "It's okay. I can fix it."

He slid down her body to take his place once more on the floor and pulled her against him.

"That won't work," she tried to tell him, but then he slipped two of his fingers into her. She arched again, the move snatching her breath away. Then his lips were there, nibbling gently on her pearl.

She ascended the mountain again as he worked his magic on her. She shifted herself to press harder against his tongue, igniting the fireworks there. Her voice joined without her even realizing, crying out in rhythm. His fingers probed deeper and twisted, exploring new angles to inspire. Arynne had never risen so high. She had never even dared to explore herself for fear of her father's and God's disapproval, but this man was meant to be her husband, even if the order of things had been changed. Destiny had united their souls, married them in spirit before they could say their vows.

That thought sent her over. Her climax burst from within, and she arched against it. She closed her eyes as her mouth remained open in a silent scream, the breath unable to escape her as her whole body contracted. Still, he continued, coaxing burst after burst of mind-numbing pleasure from her, and at last, she understood. She understood what it meant to be human and natural, the way her body had been created to bring such peace and bliss to itself. Everything she had been told about herself had been a lie.

She was beautiful, whole, and complete.

As the echo of bliss washed over her like a lapping wave, she relaxed into the bed. Her legs fell away where they had clenched together around her lover's head. She couldn't keep her eyes open. Grogginess replaced the rush of adrenaline, and she just wanted to curl up like a little girl and snuggle away from the world.

Thomas stood then and easily picked her up, sliding his arms under her neck and legs, so he could turn her the proper direction in the bed. The cool sheets pulled over her damp body, and she sighed peacefully.

Then he pulled away. Languidly, she reached out for him, but he escaped her reach. “No, don’t. Stay here,” she said with the sleepy whine of a child preparing to pout.

“Shhhh,” he hushed, laying his hand on her arms and tucking her back under the sheets. “You get some rest. I have to go clear up one more thing for our escape.”

“What is it?” she asked, concern overriding her deep exhaustion.

“Don’t worry,” he assured. “I chartered a plane to take us off this island, but I haven’t gotten confirmation yet that everything is settled. I’m going to go check and then come right back. We fly out in the morning. Get some sleep.”

She relented, setting aside her concerns. “I don’t know how I can sleep at all. I’m so excited,” she said, even as her eyes fell closed.

He patted her hands a few moments more before withdrawing. She slitted her eyes as she watched him move through the room, then go to the door. For one brief flash of light from the hall, she saw his perfect face with his dark hair and blue eyes.

“I love you,” she called out. He hesitated, pausing on the threshold, then nodded and smiled as he pulled the door shut.

It was alright that he hadn’t said it back. Her father never said those three words either, but she knew that Thomas did. Thomas loved her. He told her with his actions, and that was good enough for her.

2

Arynne didn't really think anything was wrong when she woke up alone. At first, she couldn't even remember where she was. It wasn't her bedroom at home; the hotel room was minuscule in comparison. The doors to the balcony were open with a soft, warm breeze blowing the lacy curtains inward with the coming dawn.

She remembered then. The memory of Thomas standing on the balcony framed by the colors of the setting sun, now reversing with the dawn.

"Thomas?" she called out as the events of the night before came back to her. She was still naked under the sheets, and her body buzzed from the delights she had experienced. Concluding he must have risen before her and gone to the bathroom, she got up and found her sundress, then dropped it back onto the bed in an inspiration of flirty mischief.

"Thomas?" she asked as she pushed the bathroom door slowly open only to realize immediately when the lights clicked on automatically that he had not, in fact, been inside.

She availed herself of the facilities and came back out, this time slipping the dress back on.

"Thomas?" she called out a little louder. A bang out in the hallway answered her, and she went to the door and pulled it open. An older man walked past. He started at her abrupt presence, but continued on, dragging a worn suitcase with a squeaky wheel after him. In one hand, he carried a hotel breakfast voucher.

"Sorry," she muttered and shut the door, wondering if in fact Thomas had gone down to the hotel breakfast. She tried to think if he was the coffee-drinking type. "That must be it," she said out loud to herself and scurried about the room to finish getting dressed and find her room key.

With shoes on her feet, underwear on her body, and room key in hand, she hurried down the two stories of stairs, too urgently impatient to wait for the elevator. Her breasts bounced with each gallop that she took, and she was glad no one else was on the stairs to see that. The stairwell was lined with large windows, giving a lovely view of the ocean beyond, and the sun had risen well above it, making the water shine bright and brilliant blue.

Thomas had said they would be leaving in the morning, and it was already later than she would have thought prudent, but she didn't actually know when they were supposed to fly out. She'd need to ask Thomas for all the details to settle her mind, just as soon as she found him.

She beat the older man to the lobby and startled him a second time as she burst out of the stairwell. Arynne didn't care as she scanned the room for some sign of her love. A family of parents and rowdy kids had taken over much of the lobby with their bags and bodies, and the ruckus made it really hard to scan all the faces. The father was arguing with the clerk behind the desk while several other business-attired people exited the elevator and marched into the breakfast room, separated by a pair of standing tropical plants from the rest of the lobby. Others were lining up for taxis and shuttles. When she determined that Thomas wasn't in the lobby, Arynne turned to the breakfast nook.

The dozen or so business-suited people were attacking the breakfast buffet, moving about and churning the space which again made it difficult to see anything clearly. A pair of harried waiters danced among the mostly full seats of other guests in various stages of their breakfasts. Some of the patrons looked up at her with curious eyes, but none of them stopped what they were doing—eating, conversing, or ignoring her completely—as they read their newspapers.

None of them was Thomas.

A tiny, worried squeak escaped her as Arynne turned back to the front desk, now cleared of the rambunctious family. They had emptied themselves out of the hotel and onto a shuttle bus.

The front desk clerk didn't look up at first, busying himself at the computer installed into the service desk. A second clerk stood a few feet back leaning against the back wall, looking down at his phone, completely ignoring her. Unlike the clerk at the desk, his suit was missing a tie and the top button was free. If the one at the desk was from a Men's Warehouse catalog, the other had dropped out of Prada.

"Um, sir?" Arynne tried, her voice coming out too small to get the other clerk's attention. But she didn't want to call out any louder or draw any other attention to herself. While it was not possible that anyone else in the hotel lobby area could possibly know who she was or what she had done, her emotions were running things, and they were sure that everyone knew. Everyone was judging her.

She just needed to find Thomas, and then everything would be alright.

A tiny whimper escaped her as she worried her lower lip with her teeth. Arynne clutched the edge of the desk in her rising panic of the thing she didn't dare let herself think.

At last, the desk clerk finished, and looked up with hooded, judgy eyes. "Yes, ma'am. Can I help you?" he intoned.

"Yes, have you seen ... my fiancé?" She gestured with her hand a head higher than her own. "He's about this tall, black hair, blue eyes."

The clerk sighed. "Room number?" he asked.

She had to look down at the key card in her hand with the number written on the back to remember it. A few more anxious moments passed as she waited for the clerk to look it up in his computer, though she had no idea what he would find there. She plucked at her painted nails, her manicure long overdue for a refresh.

She had no idea what could have happened.

You know what is happening. You just don't want to admit it, her inner voice whispered.

"Yes," the clerk said, interrupting her thoughts. "Your ... fiancé," he said as if he didn't believe it for one minute, "checked out of the hotel last night."

"What?" she asked in a small voice.

Her squeak didn't disturb the clerk in the slightest as he continued. "Yes, he checked out early and stated that you would be here until tomorrow." The clerk examined something on his screen. "I have a note here from the night clerk that he left you something. One moment."

The clerk turned and went into the back room. It was all that Arynne could do to hold on to the edge of the counter. The world kept spinning as she tried to gasp for air. Light became brighter, and all she could feel was her heart pounding too fast. She had a brief thought that she was going to pass out. Then off in some distant, too-remote part from herself, she heard banging and thumping of something tumbling. Then everything went black.

She had no idea how much time had passed, but she woke up lying on the ground in a circle of people. A circle of strangers.

There was no sound at first as she stared up at the faces looking down. She wondered if she had died, and it was just her soul staring up from her body, unable to think or move.

And then sound came back quickly.

"Miss, can you hear me?" the older man she had scared twice asked. He had a stethoscope in his ears and pressed the end into her chest, listening.

"Should we call an ambulance?" the informal clerk asked.

"No!" Arynne choked out weakly.

"I don't think that's necessary," the older man said. "She's just hyperventilated. I think she'll be alright."

"Why would she do that?" a woman's voice asked.

"Not surprised," the desk clerk said dryly and full of judgement. "I think her lover just abandoned her."

There were gasps from the group, *all* reacting as if she couldn't hear or see any of them.

"Oh, the poor thing," the woman said while another woman stared down disapprovingly, crossed herself, and muttered something under her breath.

"Thank you, everyone, for all your help," the informal clerk said, as if only just then realizing the scene this was all making.

"Here. I brought some water," a teenager said, belatedly joining the group, brandishing a bottle of water like it was a club.

The older man, presumably a doctor, took it from the kid before he himself got knocked in the head with it. Several of the other guests allowed themselves to be shooed away by the desk clerk, and soon the world was less overwhelming.

"Do you think you want to sit up?" the doctor asked her gently, at last meeting her eyes and looping his stethoscope around his neck while offering her a gentle smile.

"I can't go to the hospital," Arynne repeated insistently.

"Don't worry. You won't go anywhere you don't want to," the doctor assured and helped her up to sitting. The world spun for a second, and she thought she might fall back down again, but the wave of nausea washed over her. The bottle of water pressed into her hand, and she took it. Someone had already spun off the cap, so she just brought the liquid to her lips and sucked it down. The nausea abated to the low roil from before.

"Just breathe easily. No sudden movements," the informal clerk assured, rubbing her back with his open palm. She wished he wouldn't, but there was nothing she could do to stop him. She could barely feel herself as it was.

"Can we get her off the floor? She's in the middle of everything," the desk clerk asked tersely, looking around with a professional smile as he nodded and assured other guests who had just entered the lobby that everything was alright.

But it wasn't. Nothing was all right. Arynne's ears began to ring again.

Stop it, her uncharitable inner voice chided. *You're making a scene.*

"Do you think you can stand?" the doctor asked, and Arynne nodded numbly. She swallowed again and set a grip around her heart, digging for her will to stand. She couldn't give up yet.

"I need to go. I need to get out of here," she said meekly. She had a vague notion that if she just hurried and got to the airfield, maybe there was still time. She could maybe catch Thomas before his plane took off and...

Except he was already gone.

He left her last night.

Hours ago.

His plane would have already taken off.

The older doctor and the informal clerk leveraged her to her feet, each grabbing an elbow to help her stand. She wavered for a terrible moment, and she thought her legs would give out. What was happening to her? Was she dying? She felt like she was dying.

"Bring her this way. She can sit in the office," the desk clerk insisted, gesturing behind the desk.

"Got it. Can you walk?" the informal clerk asked, his cologne wafting over her as he slid an arm across her back and threaded her own arm over his shoulders. The smell should have been delicious—it was the same as Thomas's—but now it added to her sick feeling. She wanted this stranger to stop touching her, but she also didn't trust her own legs to work.

"Get her out of here!" the desk clerk insisted, even more urgently as a new group of business-clad people burst from the elevators to swamp the breakfast nook.

"Alright, alright. Calm down," the informal clerk chided under his breath.

Arynne found herself dragged to the office door behind the desk, whether she wanted to go or not. She dropped unceremoniously into a bucket chair before a large desk. Her bottle of water appeared on the edge of it next to her, half-filled now. She didn't remember letting it go. Once she sat, the informal clerk went back out the door, leaving her alone with the presumed doctor.

"Well," the doctor said, straightening beside her. "I do hate to abandon you like this, my dear, but I have to catch my flight out of here. I hope you'll be alright?" It was a question. Arynne heard the upward inflection, but she knew he wasn't really asking.

Still, she gave a token nod like a good girl. "Thank you. Thank you, doctor. I'm sorry to have been a bother," she managed to get out.

He smiled pityingly and patted her shoulder once more. Then he left with all the alacrity of a man who really didn't want to get involved.

She didn't blame him. She didn't want to be involved, and it was her life.

Just then the door opened, and the informal clerk reappeared. He thrust an envelope in her direction. Arynne stared uncomprehendingly at first.

"This is for you," he insisted, waggling the envelope at her. "This is what was left for you by your ... the gentlemen you came with."

A message! From Thomas!

At last, there would be some explanation for what was happening. Something wonderful and reasonable, and she had overreacted for nothing.

That thought infused her with new energy. She grabbed the envelope and tore the top open. The envelope had been thick, and she didn't really comprehend why until she saw the stack of bills inside. There were two bundles, each bound together with a paper band around the middle.

"Oh, gods," she creaked out as she pulled one of the two bundles out. Hundred-dollar bills bound together by a band printed with the number $5,000 on it blurred as her eyes filled with tears. She did nothing to stem them. Just let them flow down her cheeks in hot trails. "Oh, gods."

But the gods didn't seem to hear. How could this be happening to her? After everything she had risked, not just for Thomas but for herself. She had given up everything. Her life in her father's house, the comforts his money had bought her, the prestige of being his daughter, albeit without much freedom outside her gilded surroundings...

And this was all she had been worth to the man she had loved with her entire being, whom she had sacrificed everything for.

Ten thousand dollars.

Refusing to accept that was all, Arynne dug through the envelope for something more. She found it and wished almost immediately she hadn't.

Dear Arynne, the note inside read, written on a thin piece of hotel stationary. *I'm sorry, but I am not taking you with me. This should be enough money to get you back home. Take care of yourself.*

The bastard didn't even bother to sign it.

"I can't go back. I can't," she said out loud, her voice thick. Not after everything she had done. Not after her betrayal. Her father would never forgive her or worse. She didn't want to admit what her father was capable of. She had willfully ignored it most of her life, believing that ignorance would keep her safe, because she was his daughter and that was enough.

She looked up at the hotel clerk, who had continued to stand there, regarding her. She saw it in his eyes. This man knew who she was and knew who she belonged to. In a panicked motion, the clerk lifted his hands to ward her gaze off.

"This is none of my business," he said and immediately left, repeating, "This is none of my business. I'm not getting involved. I'm sorry."

And he left her alone in his office, slowly dying inside.

3

Arynne got herself back up to her room and stayed there for the rest of the day. Maybe longer. She lost track. Sometimes she slept. She definitely ignored the knocks of housekeeping, and at some point, one of the clerks reluctantly came to the room and asked her if she would be remaining beyond her allotted time, presenting her with a bill.

"The bastard didn't even pay?" she muttered, making the informal clerk flinch. She supposed it was the first sign of fire she had displayed during the whole of their short acquaintance.

"He paid for the last two days yes, but your check out time was hours ago," he stated formally. Just business.

She went to the envelope, which she had dropped beside the bed when she had flung herself on to it, and removed several of the bills. She threw them at the clerk. They sprayed around the horrible man in an explosion of paper.

"Just leave me alone," she snapped at him and slammed the door in his face. She barely got the door shut before sobs wracked from her body. She felt like she was dying, and she hoped she would. Arynne had heard of people dying of broken hearts. She prayed it would happen to her soon.

Except it didn't.

For six weeks, she stayed in the hotel, hiding in the room and occasionally ordering meals when she got an appetite to eat. Every so often, one of the clerks would reappear, and she would pass them more money to make them go away. She didn't care. Not about anything.

At least, not until the day she threw up.

Then a new terror tore through her.

"No, no, no, no," she repeated over and over as she went down to the front desk.

The informal clerk was on duty that time, and he was dressed even more informally than usual, wearing a button-down shirt with a jacket.

The clerk's eyebrows popped up in surprise at seeing her out of her room and dressed in one of the complimentary robes they had left in the room. Feeling self-conscious, she pulled the belt around herself, glancing around to see who spied her. They were thankfully alone at the moment, though she could hear people moving about down the first floor halls.

"You're still here?" he asked, surprised.

She didn't know what to say to that. She stood there awkwardly.

The clerk looked around, but there was no one else in the lobby who could help him. Or help her for that matter. "Uh, what can I do for you, ma'am?" the clerk finally asked. At least he was treating her appearance in a bathrobe with bedroom hair as normal, but he probably saw a lot of crazier things working in a hotel.

"I need—" But she stopped, loathe to say what she needed. Now that she was there, admitting what she thought out loud seemed unthinkable.

He continued to regard her, his hand resting on top of the handle of a suitcase, the other waiting on the keyboard of the hotel computer. He was obviously in the middle of something, probably helping someone with lost luggage or something. Arynne didn't care. It was a strange detail to get hung up on considering how her life was falling apart. Still, he waited patiently for her to tell him her request. The seconds drew out to awkwardness, and Arynne considered simply walking away and going back to her room when he sighed and dropped his head before taking a sharp breath through his nose. He lifted his head again and gave a small grunt. "If you give me a minute to finish this, I can drive you to the drug store before they close," he said with resigned reluctance.

Arynne's eyebrows shot up. "How do you—"

But his face said it all. He *did* know what she came to ask. She was both relieved and horrified.

He cleared his throat, his reluctance so evident, but she couldn't let him off the hook now that he offered. Her need was too great.

"Go get ready. I'll meet you down here," he said, then continued typing at the computer.

"Thank you," she whispered, then turned to go back to her room to get changed. As she got dressed, she just kept telling herself that she would go and find out, and then it would be over, and she wouldn't have to worry about it.

As she picked up the envelope of money, however, she realized how thin it had become. A quick count turned out to be too quick. Her time of wallowing in self-pity and remorse had passed, and she hadn't died from a broken heart. She stuffed what remained in the envelope into the pocket of her light jacket. Thomas had left her suitcase, so she had all the clothes she had hastily packed before the escape. Somehow, it felt better to put on her purple cargo capris that cinched at her knee if she wanted them to and her gray shirt of her favorite band.

It began to rain by the time she got downstairs to the lobby. The clerk had disappeared with the suitcase, so Arynne went out to sit in one of the wicker chairs under the covered overhang of the hotel. This was the first time she had been outside in over six weeks, and she felt like a different person sitting there watching the patter of the rain.

She let her mind wonder what Thomas was doing right then. Was he thinking of her? Did he miss her as much as she missed him?

She had gone over every memory she shared with Thomas, looking them over in every possible light and examining every yellow flag she had ignored. Also a few red flags she had denied were red.

"How could I have been so stupid?" she asked the rain. It chattered back but had no answers.

At last, the desk clerk came out of the hotel, shrugging on a black trench coat that looked like it belonged in a New York City mobster movie. Then he set a black cowboy hat on his head, that shifted the look of the trench coat entirely.

"My car is over here," he called, gesturing with keys he pulled out of his pocket.

Arynne started at that, realizing she had expected him to go get his car and pull up so she could minimize getting wet, but why would he do that? She wasn't the lady heiress anymore who was owed such favors. What he was doing was a favor in and of itself.

She pushed up from the deep-set chair and hurried after him, the rain hitting her hard on the top of her head, wetting her completely down before she had gotten half a dozen steps. They scurried together to get into his car, the headlights chirping at him as he approached. As soon as they were inside, their breath misted up the windshield.

With her hands, she slicked back her hair while he pushed the starter button on the car, dropping his keys with the attached car fob into the cup holder between them.

"Buckle up," he ordered as he did the same, crossing the belt over himself. The lightning flashed above them, blinking the world inside the car out with a burst of light. She almost jumped with it and told herself not to read into it as a bad omen.

"Thank you," she said as she clicked her buckle into place.

He had already started backing up, his focus out his rear window. "What?" he asked distractedly.

"Thank you for doing this for me," she said.

"I have a cousin," he said as if that explained everything, "and a mother. They would never speak to me again if I didn't. Not that they would anyway."

They pulled out onto the road from the hotel parking lot, but it was more like pulling out into a river.

"You don't talk to either of them?" Arynne asked, not so much because she wanted to know, but she feared them lapsing into tense silence.

"Not since..." he started to say, then stopped. "Never mind."

And then they did lapse into tense silence.

"Well, I'm sorry to hear that," she finally said after a pause more pregnant than she was. Or might be. Dammit, she didn't want to think about it. "You are a very nice man."

He shifted uncomfortably in his seat. "Thank you," he responded politely.

They stopped at an intersection. The road across from them was a sharp hill, and rain poured down it like a waterfall. Arynne had never seen anything like it. She leaned forward, breathing a wow as she watched the cascade of water.

"Whoever lives up there is stuck for a while," she said out loud, imagining what it would be like to try and skate down the slick road. Skate was probably the exact right word for it.

"You're not from this island?" the clerk asked.

She sat back to look at him, realizing she didn't even know his name. Had he been wearing a name tag? She certainly couldn't see it now because of his coat—if he still wore the tag since he'd left work.

"It's Dion," he said, catching her looking for the tag on his chest.

"What?" she asked.

"My name. It's Dion," he repeated, giving her a sideways look, like he was measuring her reaction.

"I know," she lied, embarrassed. It was obvious that she was lying, but he didn't call it out. "My name is Arynne."

"I know," he said. Of course, he knew. This may not have been her father's island, but her family name had reach. It would only be a matter of time until they found her.

But she wasn't going to talk about all that. "And no. I'm not from this island."

"Well, up the hill is where all the Richie Riches live with their private mansions," he said, finally getting to his point.

She looked up at the cascading hill as if she could see through the earth to the elaborate mansions she could imagine above. "Got it. Stay away from there," she muttered, then realized that thought *had* been out loud.

Again, Dion gave her a side eye, but again, he kept his thoughts to himself about it.

Finally, they arrived at the drugstore, its lights bright and cheery in the gloom.

"I'll wait here," he said, sliding into a parking spot. He threw the brake on too hard, and the car lurched them a bit.

But Arynne just sat there.

"This is it," Dion prompted again, gesturing to the drugstore.

"What if I *am* pregnant?" The question burst out of her in panic, like it had ripped itself right out of her chest and sat on the dashboard, an ugly twisted but no less true thing.

She stared at Dion, her only lifeline in the whole world, even if he was a reluctant one.

His eyes were wide as he stared at her, not shocked at the question so much as she had asked it. So much understanding passed between them in that tense silence. Then he blew out a breath and flopped back into his seat. "Well, you can't keep staying in a hotel."

"No, I can't," she agreed.

"How much money do you have left from what he gave you?"

She slid the envelope out of her pocket to pass to him.

He fingered through it, then whistled through his teeth. "I was afraid of this. You don't even have enough to pay off what you still owe on your rooms."

She jumped at that. "But I was paying you as we went."

"Not for the last three days. I checked in the computer," he said, looking up into the middle distance through the rain filled windshield. Then he thrust the envelope back to her. "Go in and get what you need. Then we'll go get dinner."

"Really?" she asked, suddenly feeling very uncomfortable. Images of being solicited or even forced into a compromising position passed through her. Many of them wore the faces of the men who used to work for her father. They would always promise all kinds of things: gifts, dinners, travel, and such when her father wasn't looking or listening. The price for such things was always implied, but it had never been one she had any desire to pay.

Not until Thomas.

Her father had been no help either. He had been more likely to come down on her to not tempt the men and be a virtuous, good girl. Now all she could think was if only she had listened, she wouldn't have been in this circumstance at all. She glanced nervously at the man in whose car, and therefore power, she sat in. "I... I don't..." but she had no idea how to speak without upsetting him. "I don't want—"

The tone in her voice caught his attention. He glanced back at her with a curved eyebrow, which then shot up with the other one as he realized what she was thinking. "Oh gods, no! I have absolutely no interest in..." He shook his head hard. "No, no. Just no. That's not what this is."

"You shouldn't help me," Arynne said, her voice low. "You should actually stay far, far away from me." She eyed him sideways. "You do know who I am, right?"

"No. Who are you?" he asked.

That actually made her flinch. "What? But I... I had been so certain... You really *don't* know who I am?"

His face gave nothing away, but his eyes held no obfuscation. They just searched her face for the answers to her questions. "You are a young woman who came to a hotel with a man, and that man left her in a lurch."

She narrowed her eyebrows. Was he being coy or was he truly ignorant? She decided she needed to be sure. "You *do* know who my father is?" she stressed, leaning forward.

But Dion shook his head. "No, I don't."

"Oh gods," she muttered turning away from her ignorant helper to look out the rain-streaked window. "Then... then you really should stay away from me. He's ... not a good man. And he may be my father, but ... I can't go back there again." Not after what she had done. She couldn't bring herself to say that last part.

But he wouldn't leave it alone. "Why can't you go back there... go home?" he asked softly.

She huffed. "Look, I appreciate what you have done for me, but you are better off staying far, far away from me. For your own good." She reached for the door handle and popped it open. The sound of rain rushed in through the crack as she prepared to exit the vehicle.

"Now hang on," Dion said, holding his hand out over her leg but not quite touching her. "Just hold on—"

"No, thank you. You have helped me more than enough. Thank you, really," Arynne said, and she pulled her hood back up over her head before exiting the car into the pouring rain to rush through it to the store.

4

The store lights flickered over the door as Arynne marched in, which gave an air of sickliness to the place. There were several shelves filling the room but no actual people. The clerk sat behind the counter, but they had a hand propped up on a fist and appeared to be sleeping sitting up. Arynne rubbed at the mildewy smell that tickled her nose and turned to head to the shelves.

Gratefully, she found what she sought in the farthest corner of the store. Picking up the pack that said "Oracle" on it, she turned it over to read the instructions on the back. One test should have been as good as another, but the normal act of reading the instructions was something to focus her mind on and away from the exchange that had just happened. *Those* thoughts continued to pound at her though, making it hard to actually read. Her hands shook so badly, she dropped the package.

Dion caught it.

She gasped. She hadn't sensed him approaching her.

"What are you doing?" she hissed. "You need to get away from me."

"Arynne, I—"

She snatched the package from him. "I mean it, you need to get away from me. Get as far away as you can. Nothing good is going to happen to you if you keep trying to help me. You should never have even brought me here to this pharmacy."

"Because your father could do something to me," he said, filling in the rest of her statement.

"Yes," she hissed even softer.

"Why would he do that?"

She double blinked, unprepared to give an answer. She knew why but hadn't thought about it or even articulated it for herself, never mind to a complete stranger.

"The... the less you know, the better," she said, then almost laughed at the cliché of that line. But it was true. "After what I've done, anybody who helps me will be—" Then she stopped, realizing that she had violated her own "the less you know, the better" policy in the same breath.

"I don't care," Dion said.

She huffed a dry laugh. "You don't care?" She cocked an incredulous eyebrow at him. "If you knew who my father was, you would care very much—"

"I don't care who your father is—"

"And if you knew what I had done—"

"I don't care about what you've done—"

"Or what he will do to me when he catches me—"

"I won't let anything happen—"

"Ha! You can't stop him—"

"I'm not afraid—"

"I'm trying to save you!"

She pushed him then, forcing him to take a sudden step back and cutting off the argument at the same time. For one panicked moment, she glanced up to see if they had awoken the clerk, but the clerk hadn't twitched a muscle since they came in.

Arynne looked away and noticed that at some point she had dropped the Oracle box onto the floor. She bent to pick it up, but the water in her eyes blurred it. Instead, she pressed her hands against her eyes, which only made the tears spill out faster, tears she had thought had all dried up. She sensed rather than saw Dion crouch down beside her, his presence coming around her like a shield. The temptation to sink into that presence felt so strong.

"I'm so scared," she confessed, which came out more like a sob. "I was so stupid."

"Arynne," Dion said softly. The tips of his fingers came to rest on her shoulder, conveying he wanted to hold her, but recognizing he did not have permission to touch her yet.

She looked up at him helplessly. He had knelt on one knee, the other crooked to create a wall with his coat, like he was ready to spring into action at any moment. Heat from his body wafted toward her, inviting her in. And that was what she wanted. To feel safe again and not alone.

"You're a good man," she said. "You don't deserve any of this."

He snickered at that. "I'm not so good," he assured her. "And I'm here now. So just tell me... what did you do? Why can't you go home?"

She didn't have the strength to resist anymore. "I betrayed my family. I..." She took a stuttering, hitching breath. "I used my private access and helped Thomas destroy our private security system, the Labyrinth, so that he could access—" But she stopped, realizing she had given no context to what she was saying. "My father is—" But she stopped at that, too. "Honestly, I don't really know *what* he does. I just know that it is very important that he does it securely, and that if that security was breached, it would be very, very bad. A lot of money is at stake, and the program I created protected it."

"And you helped this Thomas breach it?"

"Yes," Arynne said softly. Somehow saying it out loud made it easier to think about. "I did. He took what he wanted and then destroyed ... something inside it... Something he called the Minotaur." Arynne shook her head. "It doesn't matter. I don't really know what it was all about, and I don't really *want* to know." She swallowed. "Bad things tend to happen to people who know. I just wanted to get out of there. Get away from it all. I'm sorry I can't tell you what—"

"It's fine. I don't really care about what," Dion assured.

Arynne sniffed at that. "Thomas did. He would ask me all kinds of questions about it." She pressed her hands over her face in regret. "He was manipulating me, wasn't he? Pumping me for information, just like in those movies, and I, like an idiot, just..."

"Hey, hey," Dion said softly, taking her hand away from her face and holding it warm within his own. "This is not your fault."

"Don't say that." She shook her head. "It doesn't change anything. When my father finds me—"

"He won't."

"Stop saying that. Of course he will," she said, getting angry now. "He will. He can, and he will. Then it won't even matter that I'm..." She stopped as that thought dawned on her. "God, I'm so stupid. How can I say I don't know what he was doing—then why would I be so afraid, right? I know that what he is doing is bad, and that it matters more to him than my life. Or yours."

"Like I said, I'm not afraid."

She looked up into his warm eyes. "You should be."

He shrugged one shoulder. "Arynne, I have an idea. An idea of what we can do to keep you safe and solve all your other immediate problems."

Just like that, her shields went back up. She may not have known what her father was involved in, but she was her father's daughter and saw the danger in that statement. But she was also desperate. "What is it?" she asked cautiously.

"There is a job... One of the houses up on Richie Rich hill need a caretaker. You'll be all alone up there, but it comes with a salary, and you can live in the house and everything," he said. "I bet I can even get you benefits. You know, like insurance and stuff. Your father will never find you."

Arynne didn't believe that was true. "He can find me anywhere."

"Look, he doesn't know where you, and this Thomas guy escaped, too, right?" Dion reasoned. "And even if he did, and say it did lead him to the hotel, all they will know is that Thomas left without you. Your name wasn't on the reservation, and all any of the eyewitnesses still here can attest to is you left a few weeks later, but no one would necessarily know where, right? You've talked to nobody."

"Except you," she stated.

"Except me," he agreed.

"And then they find my body buried under concrete decades later," she muttered.

That surprised him. "I'm not ... not a serial killer," he said, popping up an eyebrow at her as if asking if she was making a joke or an accusation.

"I've already had one mysterious man make me promises I wanted to hear," she said.

Dion shrugged. "I don't know what to tell you, Arynne. I know we just met, but I do sincerely want to help you."

"Why?"

He hesitated a moment. "Would it make sense to you that you remind me of someone that I failed to help once?"

"Someone?" she questioned, not giving him an inch.

"My mother," he said quietly with the edge of a death knell. She knew without being told that she was dead.

She looked down at the Oracle box in her hand. She had someone else to care for now. She knew it without even taking the test. "The security camera footage behind the desk would—" she started to say.

"Yeah, but I'll make sure it gets erased. We can cover your tracks. We can even change your name. Or rather your last name. I think your first name is very pretty."

"Don't," she stated with more force than she intended. "Don't say something like that to me."

His eyebrows shot up, but he held his hands up in surrender. "I apologize. I didn't mean—"

"I don't care what you meant. I don't want any of that, at all. I'm not trading anything, not my body, not anything for that. So, if that is what this is really about, then you need to walk out that door and leave me the hell alone." Some of the imperious princess she used to be reasserted itself again, the one that could command respect in a room full of men with lustful eyes and disgusting thoughts. She was sure it would put this would-be savior off and show his true intentions, but he only nodded as if it was what he was expecting to hear.

"Agreed," he said simply.

"Good," she said.

"Shall we get that and go to dinner?" he said, nodding at the box in her hands. "We can work out any other details then."

Still, she hesitated.

He sighed. "Sometimes you have to give the world a radical 'yes' when it tries to help you."

"That's stupid," she said, shaking her head.

"Then *I'm* stupid. I have said 'yes' to everything in my life when it has been offered. Let me do the same for you. Please."

"Yes, alright," she agreed. After all, what other choice did she have?

5

Walking through the front door of the estate house felt like walking into her old home. Well, her father's home. At least the one on his private island.

Still, Arynne's mouth gaped as she stared across the marble floor to the twin grand staircases that arched upward on either side of the foyer. The walls and floor were all built from cream-colored marble, including the fountain in the middle of the floor up to the Romanesque columns with bright wood rafters high above. The fountain itself looked like four giant sake cups placed within four open squares that were supposed to hold water but, at the moment, held air. It felt more like a hotel lobby than a home and yet more welcoming than any hotel she had ever been in. Debris was everywhere.

"This... this is so ... grand," Arynne breathed as she turned in place to look at the finely appointed walls. The whole space was one large circle and around the top was a balcony that ringed the place leading to various doors she could only see the tops of from the ground.

"Yeah, I suppose it is," Dion said, obviously not thinking much of it as he walked in behind her. He stopped at a small table by the door to drop the keys he had used to open it. He sniffed as he spun in his own circle, taking in the piles of old leaves and other gatherings of plant matter in the corners.

"The original owner, or maybe their caretaker or something, just left the door standing open and..." He gestured at the mess. "The jungle has tried to reclaim it."

"It just needs cleaning," Arynne said, already defending the place as if it were her own.

She loved it. She absolutely loved it. Arynne didn't care about its neglect; the sweeping architecture of the place was beautiful underneath all of the grime and neglect.

Walking up to the edge of the fountain, she looked inside one of the "cups." Something had obviously made a nest there, having piled leaves and sticks around the inner edges of the bottom. She could imagine something furry with a tail curling up in the center comfortably.

"So, it's furnished," she said, moving past the fountain to a pair of couches, a cluster of armchairs, and a dining table each in their own little setting and all positioned before three picturesque windows.

The window straight ahead looked out at a pool of water framed with greenery on the brink of breaking past its boundaries. The one window to the right had a view of the ocean instead, while the window to the left seemed more like an island jungle. The house stood situated on a small inlet at the edge of the larger island. The view created an illusion that the mansion sat on an island all by itself. Despite the glorious view, the sky outside hung gray with the current storm, spitting rain down to make the pool outside dance.

Dion had drifted over to what looked like a well-appointed kitchen off to the right of the "dining area." He stepped up and around the long bar-like counter lined with high backed stools that were only partially covered by a white sheet meant to protect them. He went straight to the sink and turned on the tap. Nothing came out.

"Okay, so they turned the water off. Not a surprise, but we'll need to find the main shut off valve for the house and see if the whole system works."

Arynne grinned. "You know something about plumbing?"

"I know basics about plumbing," he said. "When you can't afford a plumber, you get very handy."

He went to the fridge next and opened it to look inside. A light clicked on, revealing nothing much except an empty Tupperware container and a bottle of something that had separated into its respective parts long ago. Dion immediately took the bottle out and dropped it into the empty garbage can nearby. "And we will definitely need to restock if you decide to stay."

"Of course, I've decided to stay. I have nowhere else to go. I just can't believe someone would abandon a place like this so callously," she said. Somehow, Arynne felt more like herself here than she had since Thomas abandoned her. But she had to stop thinking about that now. She needed to focus on her and the baby.

She may have failed at everything else in her life, but she couldn't fail now.

"Do you know much about cleaning and repairing?" Dion asked.

Arynne stiffened her jaw. "I can learn. How hard can it be?" she said.

Dion sniffed at that but said nothing. She got worried. After all, perhaps the owners of this place would want to hire someone more experienced. Sure, Dion was the one telling her about this job, but the final decision wasn't really up to him, was it?

"So, the job... being a caretaker," she started, gesturing to the house, trying to figure out how to phrase her question. "I mean... am I going to have to apply for it or talk to someone or something?"

"No, don't worry. It's yours if you want it. You just have to fill out a tax form and sign an employment agreement, but it's only one page, so we can get it done now if you're sure you want it." He reached into the inner pocket of his jacket and pulled out two pieces of folded paper.

"Seriously? It's that easy?" she asked. She had never had a job before, but this seemed too simple.

"It is this time," Dion answered, holding the papers out to her while he patted his pockets. "Go ahead and look at them while I hunt down a pen. I completely forgot to grab one."

She did as he bid while he went and pulled open drawers in the kitchen to hunt for something to sign with.

The contract read straightforward enough, and she saw two lines at the bottom: one for her to sign and one for the owner of the house to sign. Both were blank.

"So, who are the owners of this place?"

"Huh, that is the question, isn't it? This place has passed through so many hands. I think the last time it went through two or three sets in the span of three hours."

"What? What do you mean?" Arynne asked, arching an eyebrow.

"It was a poker game," Dion said, giving her a half smile. "The deed ended up in several pots and everything. Full of high stakes to make a spy thriller proud." He chuckled to himself as he pulled a pen out of what looked to be a junk drawer of sorts, but Arynne didn't get the joke.

"Well, okay. But..." She blew out an exasperated breath. "Who owns it now?"

Dion cocked his head at her as if the answer should be obvious. "Oh. I do. I won the pot."

Arynne froze, then blinked as her brain rebooted with that information. "You what now?"

He chuckled. "I own this place. That's why I'm down here, trying to get the paperwork for it all sorted out. I hold the deed, but apparently there are accounts and stuff associated with this place that are not in my name and a whole bunch of other tax issues and... it's frankly a whole mess that is going to take longer than I have time for to sort out. Throw some weird legal inheritance hurdles that have to be dealt with, and you know, here we are." He held the pen out to her to take.

"But..." Arynne felt like the floor had shifted from underneath her. "But you work at the hotel ... and you own a mansion?"

He furrowed his eyebrows and cocked his head to one side. "I don't work at the hotel," he replied.

"But I saw you," Arynne said, shaking her head and pointing in the direction of the hotel. "You were behind the desk and everything. With that suitcase."

"Uh yeah, nobody was manning the desk, and I was tired, so I just started checking myself in," Dion admitted, then chuckled at himself. "I know the guy behind the desk, Zephyr. He's an old friend." He chuckled a little harder as he realized her mistake. "You thought I worked for the hotel?"

"Oh, my gods, I feel so stupid." Arynne pressed a hand over her eyes, her cheeks burning. "This whole time you were just a guy at the hotel? I... I trusted you with my deep dark secrets and you..."

"Hey, hey, what's the problem here?" Dion asked as she pulled away. "Are you saying things would be different if I worked for the hotel?"

"Well, yes! Those people, they were paid to help, and they're not like ... us, not... you know..." She realized what she was saying and how horrible it sounded, even as she understood it to be true.

Dion's jaw tightened and his mirth vanished. "What are you saying?" he challenged. "Are you really referring to Zephyr and everyone else at the hotel as a servant class?"

"No! I mean..." Except that was what she was saying, and she realized it. She felt like she was drowning, and she barely understood why.

Dion seemed to grow angrier as he crossed his arms to look down his nose at her. "So, because you're from money, little princess, that makes you better? My, how you have fallen then. Are you sure you even *want* the job? Think you can stand to *lower* yourself?" he said hotly.

Tears beaded in Arynne's eyes as she wrapped her arms around her stomach, over the baby inside her. She was screwing this up, and she knew it. But she resisted. She resisted letting the grief take her and collapse her into the "little girl" whining she wanted to do. She couldn't.

Instead, she swallowed and bowed her head. "No, I do want the job. I'm sorry. I didn't mean..."

"Yeah, you did," Dion insisted, not relenting.

She took a fortifying breath and met his eye. "I did. You're right. And I was wrong to imply it. I'm sorry. I very much want the job. Please, sir."

She waited for his response, and after a breath, something shifted in him. He dropped his arms, holding his hand out for the papers and the pen he had given her.

He was taking the offer back.

Arynne felt her stomach drop out, but she held her dignity as she passed the papers back to him. She thought he would tear them up, but instead, he turned and went back to the kitchen counter. Setting the papers down, he applied the pen and signed his name. Then turned to her, offering it back so she could do so as well.

Relieved, she took it and did so.

While she signed, he said, "I am sorry. I shouldn't have lost my temper. Who the fuck am I to judge you after everything you've been through?"

"It's alright, really," she said as she finished signing her name.

"You need to fill out the tax form, too," he said, pulling the second sheet out and pointing to the place for her name and address.

She stared at the blank a second. "But what address should I put down?"

"This one," he said, his smile returning to his face. "This is your home now."

She looked up into his face, closer to hers than she had realized. Her breath caught in her throat; a tremor skittered in her lower stomach. The smile on his face slipped into something more serious. His eyes danced over her face as if he searched for something written there. Gently, one of his fingers rose to brush back a strand of her hair. Another flush burned through her at his light touch. She hadn't felt a rush like that since ... Thomas.

Arynne flinched back, pulling away from Dion as the memory of her one true love shocked her back. What was she doing? She was pregnant with another man's child and here she was having ... feelings for someone else? Confused, she gripped the pen in her hands tightly, trying to understand what was happening. Gods, was she really so fickle as to forget how much she loved Thomas? No, she *had* loved him. It had been real. It had to be. She would never love again. Not like that.

While the torrent of thoughts tore through her, Dion cleared his throat, taking a step back. Oh gods, he was embarrassed, too. She had crossed some line. He was her employer now!

"I'm so sorry... I—" she started to say, but her voice was so soft he didn't hear.

"So, anything else you want to see in the house, or should we just bring the suitcases in?" Dion asked.

"Uh, yeah. Let's bring in the suitcases," she said and turned to go back out into the rain to the car, but Dion held up a hand to her, stopping her.

"No, it's okay. I'll get them," he said and exited quickly. Fled would be a better word for it.

"Stupid, fickle woman," Arynne said, cursing herself, unrealizing that she was repeating her father's words. Instead, she looked down at Dion's name written beside hers.

Gently, she ran a finger over it. "Dion Brewer," it said.

He came back carrying her suitcase and dragging his wetly behind him. "Okay, so what do you want to see next?" he asked.

Arynne shrugged. "Well... where are the bedrooms?"

6

"Oh, gross!" Arynne cried as the thing that reminded her of a squirrel or a rat bolted out from under the bed.

She jumped away, letting it escape out the master bedroom balcony before it kamikaze-leapt into gods-knew-where. There were plenty of trees on the island for it to find a new home.

Once Arynne got her panicked breathing under control, she swallowed the bile back down her throat.

Along with the nonspecific rodent came a rancid stench from under the bed.

She stood there for several labored breaths, praying her stomach contents would stay stomached contents. Slowly, the nausea subsided. Gripping the broom in her hands, Arynne fortified her determination and got back on her knees to thrust her weapon of cleaning under the bed once more. With one big swipe, she pulled out the nest of the invader. It smelled even worse.

This time she had to full sprint to get to bathroom in time. It took a rinse of her mouth and a small towel tied around her face before she dared go back into the main room.

"Oh gods, oh gods, oh gods, oh gods," Arynne chanted as she swept the thing into an open waiting bag one step down from the dais the bed rested on. It looked like the creature had torn a sheet to bits along with the stuffing from one of the pillows. There were even "homey touches" like leaves and twigs from the outside.

"You okay?" Dion asked as he came into the room, his arms full of freshly dried bedsheets.

"Gods no," Arynne said, pressing the back of her hand against her mouth through the towel before impolitely *urp*-ing acidy air. "Ugh, sorry."

As he got closer, Dion wrinkled his nose. "Don't be. I think I'm the one that owes you the apology." He dropped his load on the unmade mattress and bowed in half to look under the bed. "What is that?"

"Something built a nest," she replied, again fighting the urge to run to the bathroom. If she kept running there every few minutes, this was going to take longer to clean.

"Ah, okay. Great," Dion said and pushed the side of the bed, shifting it. Unfortunately, all that did was send one leg off the dais with a loud thunk. He held his hand out to Arynne. "Here. Give me the broom. I'll get this cleaned up and mopped."

"No, it's my job—" she started to protest.

"The grocery delivery just arrived, so why don't you go down and put that away instead? Might be easier on you," he suggested.

Despite her nausea, Arynne's stomach growled, which was a very strange bodily contradiction, being both hungry and nauseous. Pregnancy was fun.

"Okay, thank you," she yielded, pulling the towel from her face as she left the room.

Down in the kitchen on every available counter space were rows of paper bags filled with food, along with Styrofoam boxes packed with fresh meats and frozen items packaged among cold packs. To her surprise and relief, in the first bag she peeked into, she found a packet of Preggie Pops, little ginger candies in strawberry, orange mango, and lemon lime flavors. Sucking on one soothed her roiling insides, and she set about unpacking the rest of the kitchen, making executive decisions where everything should go.

Outside the picturesque windows, the gray world had turned back to rain as night crept in. The world inside the vaulted room was bright though. Dion had turned on every light in the main building, making the place feel warm and inviting. Outside in the gardens, lights hidden among the greenery came on automatically as things grew darker, filling their little private jungle with fairy light. The pool itself also illuminated with underwater lighting, shifting the color of the water from light blue to greens to pinks and back again.

Arynne felt better and better about her decision every moment that passed.

She was about halfway through the bags on the first counter when the front door opened and slammed shut. She started with a scream, which made the intruder startle as well with his own bellow.

"What the hell are you doing here?" he asked, shoving back the hood of his raincoat to stare at her. It was the original front desk clerk from the first day she had arrived at the hotel.

"I work ... and live here?" she said, though it came out more like a question, like she wasn't sure that was the right answer. "What are you doing here?"

“Is everything okay down there?” Dion’s voice called down over the inner balcony. The intruder looked up, presumably at Dion. “Zephyr, did you scare my caretaker?”

“More like she scared me,” the clerk named Zephyr said, shaking off his raincoat to leave it to hang dripping on the door handle. “You’re welcome, by the way.” He gestured at all of the groceries. Arynne didn’t know what to say to that, but Dion interjected.

“Come on up. I got some fresh towels up here,” he said, then disappeared back behind the rail.

Zephyr kicked off his wet shoes and sopping socks, looking more like a drowned cat with his smaller feet and hairy toes. He stuffed the socks in the shoes, picked up what looked like a guitar case that was doing a better job sloughing off the wet, and carried the whole mess with him over to one of the sweeping staircases to get up to the second floor inner balcony.

Arynne went back to unpacking groceries with a shrug.

Dion popped open the dryer situated in the maid closet on the second floor and retrieved a raging hot but dry towel from within.

“You’re taking in strays now?” Zephyr asked, coming through the door just in time to catch the towel as Dion tossed it to him.

“Mutual interest. I needed a caretaker for the place; she needed a job. It’s the universe’s doing—not mine,” Dion replied, canceling the remaining time on the dryer and pulling the rest of the towels out into a waiting basket. He then held out a hand and took Zephyr’s wet socks to throw in with the next load of towels.

His friend then thrust the guitar case out to him. "You left this at the hotel."

"Oh, thanks, man," Dion said but didn't take it, indicating the fresh towels in the basket he just picked up.

Zephyr silently accepted a towel and continued to carry the suitcase, following Dion back to the master bedroom. Dion set his basket next to the door while Zephyr came to a full stop.

"What the hell happened here?" he asked, staring at the bed that Dion had managed to shove off the dais to get at the gross smelling mess underneath.

"Had a squatter," Dion said, stepping up to move the mop bucket full of filthy water and mop away from the better smelling floor. "I think that stain is always going to be there, but nobody will see it if we just move the bed back, right?" he asked, eyeing the darker colored wood where the nest had been decaying.

"I guess," Zephyr replied, still holding the guitar. Then he sighed as he realized, "I'm guessing you want me to help you move the bed back up?"

"Ding, ding, ding. You're such a smart guy, Zeph," Dion said.

Zephyr shook his head. "I should have stayed in New York," he grumbled, setting the guitar down and crossing in his bare feet to help Dion lever the bed back up. A lot more grumbling and cursing later, they succeeded. Dion then took the dirty, smelly mop water into the bathroom to dump it down the toilet.

"I think places like this have a janitor's sink somewhere," Zephyr said as he watched through the wall. The way the room was designed was strange. The space was a sort of half circle with windows facing out toward the ocean. The bed on the dais was the focal point, but going through either door framing the bed opened into the bathroom. Half the wall between the bedroom and the bathroom was simply gone, which the designer probably did so as not to obstruct the gorgeous view while one did their business.

"Too late now," Dion said as he hit the flush lever on the toilet.

Whatever high tech design it had was more than adequate for whisking away the mop water with the speed of a jet engine. The toilet chirped a request on its side to confirm if he wanted bidet service. He ignored it, and within a few seconds, a little spray of water launched itself in a small arc then stopped.

"Okay. That was weird," he noted, then shut the lid of the toilet.

"What's weird is why did you hire a caretaker if you're going to do all the cleaning yourself?" Zephyr asked as he came back out of the bathroom.

"Well, she needs somewhere to sleep, and there is a ton of work," Dion answered pleasantly, picking up the bedsheets he had brought in earlier to start making the newly relocated bed.

Zephyr shot him a raised eyebrow. "And this is why you've checked out of the hotel?"

"Well, I can't let her stay here all alone," Dion argued, but he heard how it sounded.

Zephyr shook his head. "For gods' sake, Dion. She's pregnant with another man's child. You have no idea what kind of baggage you are getting into—"

"Yes, thank you, Zephyr," Dion said with the stiff politeness that implied a warning.

"Dude... just," Zephyr blew out an exasperated sigh. "What if she later claims *you're* the father? The timing here is very suspicious. I mean, I know it isn't yours, but if she takes you to court or even tells the newspapers, it doesn't mean jack diddly."

"Jack diddly?" Dion repeated, grinning at the old timey turn of phrase.

"Bite me," Zephyr responded.

"I didn't realize we had that kind of relationship," Dion answered, leaning over the bed he was making to give his friend a waggle of his eyebrows.

"Gods!" Zephyr exclaimed, recoiling away. "Don't be an ass. You know if Erik were here, he'd say the same thing."

Dion's face fell at the mention of their mutual friend. Well, maybe "friend" was a strong word for it. "Yeah, well, Erik isn't here." He seized one of the pillows for the bed and roughly shoved it into a clean pillowcase. "And advice about something like this is both the last thing I would want from him of all people and really super judgy from a guy like you, considering how you throw your street cred around every chance you get."

"Not every chance," Zephyr corrected. "Only when it's to my advantage." The other man actually managed to hold a straight face for a whole ten seconds before they both cracked up in laughter.

"I'm not sleeping in here with her," Dion amended. "Not that it's any of your business."

"I just don't want to see you get ripped to shreds by the paparazzi or something."

"What? Like my dad?" Dion countered. "I'm just going to stick around until she feels safe. I got to get back for that concert anyway. So, thank you for the guitar because Ecstasy is going to kill me if I don't rehearse a little bit."

"Right," Zephyr said, still passing a critical eye over his handiwork as Dion laid out the comforter and folded it over.

"Are you staying to eat?"

"Thank you but no. I got to get back. The manager I hired has already quit, so now I have to run his shift until I can find someone else," Zephyr grumbled.

Dion barked a laugh. "At least you didn't buy a restaurant. Then you'd really be screwed."

"Next time I think it's a good idea to invest all my money into a hotel, just keep punching me in the head until I lose consciousness," Zephyr stressed.

"Will do," Dion acknowledged.

"Dion?" a small voice came from the door.

Dion felt his heart skip a beat at the sound of her voice. Arynne stood there in her Dionysus band t-shirt and jeans. His eyes caught on it every time. She looked more beautiful to him in it than if she had been in a ball gown or even naked. He swallowed before he could catch himself and got a warning grunt from Zephyr.

"Yeah?" Dion asked, ignoring his friend entirely.

"I wasn't sure what to make for dinner," she said, eyeing Zephyr.

She plucked at her shirt, lifting it to wipe away some sweat from her upper lip. It made him grin.

"What?" she asked, noticing him.

"Nothing," he said. "I just like your shirt."

"Oh, yeah," she said, dismissively, looking down at the old thing. "They're my favorite band."

"Oh, my dear lord," Zephyr said, slapping his hand over his mouth.

"What?" Arynne asked, alarmed by the reaction.

"Nothing. Nothing. Not a damn thing at all. I'm not getting involved, and I'm not staying for dinner. I actually can't," Zeph admitted. "I got to get back to the hotel as soon as my socks are done." Just then the dryer dinged faintly down the hall.

"Okay," Arynne said, then looked over at Dion, her eyebrows pursed in the middle, unsure. "And you?"

"Well, you made a good point about me not staying in my own house, so if you don't mind, I'll be in another of these rooms," he said as he walked toward her to the door, in order to lean out and indicate down the balcony hall.

"Oh, I see," she said, her face giving nothing away.

"Is that alright?" he asked, holding his breath.

"It's your house," she agreed. Then she added, "But ... shouldn't you stay in the master suite?"

He didn't have a good answer to that. It just didn't feel right to not give the lady the better room.

"He's too chivalrous for that," Zephyr said, saving him.

"Oh," Arynne said and that was all she said, her face masking her feelings again. He had no idea why he itched to pull that mask away, but he couldn't shake it. Without saying another word, she turned and went over to the metal spiral staircase that connected the balcony to the back of the kitchen area.

"Gods, you are in so much trouble," Zephyr said under his breath.

7

Arynne sat on a stool watching Dion as he moved around the kitchen, nibbling on a pack of dry saltine crackers. They were heavenly. Everything else had been put away, and their other guest had left. Now that there was a bed to fall into, she felt bone tired, but she needed to eat first. Thankfully, Dion had taken point on making them something, and so far, it looked like soup.

"Well, I think we accomplished a lot today," Dion said cheerily, like he was having the time of his life. "Cleared up two bedrooms and got the kitchen in order. That's a great start."

"Yeah," was all she could reply. It was so hard to keep her eyes open, but she tried to force her brain to work, if sluggishly. "And turned the water back on."

"Yeah, we should have some hot soon," Dion noted, turning the tap on to run his fingers under it. Within seconds, he snapped his fingers back and shook them. "Yup, we got hot water."

He turned the tap back off, shaking his fingers a little bit more to cool them. "Do you want to take the first shower?"

Arynne felt herself recoil. *The first shower?*

He did say he was staying, but it seemed strange to be talking about private domestic stuff like showering.

A flutter of anxiety tickled down her spine. *I barely know him. What if he's not what I think he is?* she thought, imagining all the evil things he could do to her.

He looked up and smiled kindly. "Or I can go back to the hotel if you'd rather?" he offered, reading her expression.

"Oh." Arynne blinked at that, scrubbing away what she was thinking from her face. "Well, it is your house."

"Yes, but I realize that you might feel uncomfortable staying with a man you barely know. I just want you to feel safe. I didn't want you to be alone out here. But you just tell me either way, Arynne."

The way he said her name felt so right and warm in his voice. She liked it. It made her feel unreasonably happy but also guilty. What would Thomas think?

"I just want you to know ... I'm not *like* that. I don't just ... sleep around with anybody, okay?" she started, struggling to phrase it in a way that didn't sound like a lie, even though it was the truth. "I only did *that* because I thought I loved him and that we were going to be together forever. I just don't want you to misunderstand."

"I know," Dion said, so simply and matter-of-factly that for a brief moment she thought he misunderstood.

"No, I mean—"

Gently, a hand covered hers. "Arynne, you don't owe me or anyone an explanation. If you want to talk about it, I'll listen, but I just want to be your friend. I don't want anything else from you. I promise. I will never touch you without your permission. Except right now, I guess," he said, retracting his hand as he realized his ironic error.

Arynne would have laughed, but the feelings held in her chest broke through. Tears dripped from Arynne's eyes, even though she thought she had shed them all weeks ago. Had it really been weeks since Thomas had left her?

"You must think I'm an idiot," she said, wiping at the tears, trying to hold it together.

"No, I don't. I think he's an asshole. From what I know of you and what I've seen, I think you loved him fiercely, and he failed to be worthy of that love."

The tears kept falling and a sob broke through. "Dammit," she said. "I don't want to feel this anymore."

Dion released her hand and came around the counter. "Can I hold you?" he asked softly. She nodded clumsily like a child, and like a child, she let him fold her into his arms. To her surprise, it didn't feel wrong or awkward. It felt good and safe. And heavy.

Dion didn't realize until she took a shuddering breath that Arynne had fallen asleep in his arms. He had heard about this phenomenon with pregnant women, the ability to instantly fall asleep, and he would have laughed except it could startle her awake. He couldn't know what she was going through, but he had a very good idea.

For a moment, he thought about carrying her upstairs to the bedroom but decided against it. If at any point she woke up in the transfer, he could see her getting the wrong idea, and he wouldn't blame her. He wanted her to feel safe. But he also couldn't stand there in that awkward crouch, propping her up on a stool for who knew how long.

Making an executive decision, he chose to risk taking her to the couch. In her sleep, she rolled into his arms and made a token effort to grab for his neck. Instead, her hands dropped onto her middle. Her head continued to pillow on his shoulder. It wasn't until he tried to transfer her to the couch that she resisted. For a brief moment, her head bobbed up, her eyes opening sleepily.

"It's okay," he said. "You are safe."

She accepted that and closed her eyes again, dropping over onto her side, barely twitching when he pulled her shoes off.

When Arynne awoke, she was warm. Pushing herself up to sitting, she found she was covered with the deep wine-red comforter they had washed from the master bedroom. The lights in the main hall were dimmed to twilight with light only coming from sconces just under the second floor balcony. Outside, it was full dark, and she had no idea what time it was other than still night. She had no memory of dreaming nor of falling asleep—just a sense of being warm and safe.

For the longest moment, she considered laying her head back down and going back to sleep, seeing if she could find a dream or two. She realized she could very easily.

But a sneaky little thought drifted into her mind. *Where is Dion?*

She couldn't ignore it. It was a good question. Obviously, he had been the one to bring her to the couch and cover her up, but how long ago was that? And weren't they about to eat dinner? What happened?

Looking around the room, she saw no sign of her benefactor. A pot sat on the stove, a pair of bowls and spoons on the counter beside it. Presumably their dinner. Otherwise, the kitchen was all cleaned up from the cooking.

Getting up, she went to the middle of the kitchen, not really feeling hungry. If anything, she felt more like a ghost, drifting around in a dream-like state, not really needing or wanting anything. Just an answer. Where was her host?

Softly, just on the edge of her hearing, came a distant sound. She held perfectly still so she could hear it better. It disappeared for a moment, then came back again. She still couldn't quite discern what it was, but she got a better idea as to what direction it came from.

Just passed the back wall of the kitchen were two entryways on either side, both connecting into a hallway beyond. She had yet to explore past the kitchen, but now she stepped down two steps and found herself in a glass hallway that connected to another building. The other building was smaller but designed exactly the same, a large, white cylinder body with a round, peaked roof of clay roofing tiles and windows all around it. The sound echoed down the glass hallway, like something was calling to her with long, musical cries. Walking through the glass hallway gave another view of the night ocean beyond. Through the glass, she could hear the waves crashing against the side of their finger of land.

The hallway emptied inside the other building, this one less open than the main one. She stood within a smaller version of the marble lobby, this one with doors all around that led off to presumably different rooms. She itched to open them all and explore, but one already stood open at the far end, letting a slice of light cut across. That was the one the sound came from, and now she could identify it. It was a man singing.

She walked to the door, her socked feet silent on the stone. As she crossed, the acoustics amplified the sound, making it feel almost like it came from all around her. Carefully, she cracked the door more open and peeked inside.

Beyond was a library like something out of a fairy tale. Unlike the rest of the place, where the palate choices of the buildings were meant to invoke a sense of tropical paradise and light, this room was filled with dark wood shelves. The floor was carpeted instead of tiled or marbled. Like the rest of the place, it rose two floors, an inner balcony ringing the second floor and two spiral staircases placed at opposite ends. And, of course, there were all the books. The books on the first floor had the repetitive, leather consistency expected on movie sets or photo shoots. The books on the second floor were more hodgepodge with every book seeming to have a different colored cover and size all mixed together, competing like flowers in a garden show for the most enticing.

In the center of the room, just beneath the farthest balcony, sat an almost obnoxiously large desk. It had a traditional lamp on one corner, throwing light all over the surface. That was it for tradition because in the middle sat a laptop computer connected to a small, violently red box that had its own vine-like cord connecting it to a guitar.

Arynne saw all of that and noted none of it as her eyes glued onto the man ... to Dion standing just off center from the desk. His back was turned to her, and for a moment, it was all she could focus on as it was broadly bare, except for the slash of a guitar strap across it. His hair moved damply as he bobbed his head, as if he had taken a shower very recently. His hair was held back with a pair of large headphones, its own swirling cord connected to the laptop. Gray cotton pants hugged his hips, obviously tied there with a cord that was starting to fail to hold, as the cloth pooled at his bare feet.

He didn't seem to notice, though. Instead, he moved and swayed to the sounds within his headphones, his fingers picking at the guitar strings but making barely any sound. Then he started to sing again.

"Words that stimulate your heart,
Have never torn us so far apart,
I know I need to get back to you-hooo-ooo.
I dreamed of all your naked parts,
Soulful dreams that couldn't start,
Without needing to get back to you-hooo-ooo."

It was the "ooo" parts she had been hearing, echoing down the hall as he danced up and down scales of notes. He turned toward the door as he sang and gyrated, but he didn't see her as his eyes were closed. His face was all planes and shadow with the desk lamp at his back, like he stood on a backlit stage.

Still feeling like she was part of a dream, Arynne drifted through the door and sat down on one of the nearby over-stuffed chairs designed for sinking into and reading. It was like she had snuck into a private concert. It felt downright naughty as she folded her hands into her lap and watched the god-like man sing. She had never been the type to moon over the images of beautiful men. She had always been privately tutored, and what socializing she had done with the daughters of other oligarchs had been polite and distant. There had been no sharing of scintillating thoughts that made one as thirsty as Arynne felt right then. She had watched television, music videos, and concerts online, streaming whatever she had been interested in, so she had an idea of these things. Yet to see a half-naked man like him doing it live, even though she could barely hear the music he made, stirred something inside her. It felt so private and intimate, with pressure burning in her chest.

And sing he did, going over the chorus and the verses of the song. A few times he opened his eyes, but he only focused on his picking as he worked out a finger combination or went over to the computer to restart his program. Then he started singing a song she recognized. Not just the tune, but the sound of his voice. He sang with a deep rolling bass that would switch in the next song to a panty-dropping baritone, then slip up to a soaring tenor that tore her heart out and inspired at the same time.

She knew that voice.

"Dionysus," she whispered to herself as she plucked at the center of her t-shirt.

8

In that moment of her realization, Dion finally turned and looked straight at her with his eyes wide open. He yelped as he startled, which ended up loosening what hold his pants had on his hips. The cloth dropped tantalizingly low before he caught it, showing that his taut belly continued flat all the way to the last minute.

Arynne's cheeks blushed and she looked away a moment, as much to collect herself as to give him a second of dignity.

"So, you woke up?" Dion asked as he covered up both literally and figuratively. "What time is it?"

"I don't really know," she admitted and stood up to come deeper into the library. She felt embarrassed now to come into the light, so she stopped a few feet away, her hands gripping the bottom edge of her t-shirt, trying to resist the urge to take it off. "I didn't realize... I didn't notice..."

What she "didn't" was know what to say. She certainly couldn't claim to be his biggest fan because if she was, wouldn't she have recognized him right away?

"Oh," he said. That "oh" was enough to get her to look up at him. "You figured it out, huh?"

"You're Dionysus. Not just Dion?" The last came out like a question.

"Well," he popped up one of his eyebrows, "technically, I'm both. My name really is Dion Brewer. And I am the lead singer of Dionysus ... the multi-platinum, multi-international hit performance artist."

He slipped the strap over his head to lean the guitar against the desk. "I wasn't meaning to keep it from you or anything. It's just one of those really awkward ways to introduce yourself, you know."

He still looked guilty. "You must think I'm awful," he said, uncoiling the headphones from his head to drop onto the desk.

"I... what? No...?" Arynne started, a little surprised. "I mean, I didn't even recognize you at first—"

"And why should you? I mean how arrogant of me, right?" Dion scoffed as he picked up a towel that he had thrown over a chair to place around his shoulders, covering his chest, like he was embarrassed. And in fact, he was. His cheeks and ears burned bright red.

"I'm literally wearing your t-shirt," Arynne said. "I mean, I know your freaking middle name, Dion Rodney Brewer. You're from Minnesota in the US, and your first single went triple platinum the same year your mother..." She pulled up short.

"The same year my mother died," he finished for her. "And I brought her back to life again with that song, immortalizing her in the annals of music legend forever, right behind 'Stairway to Heaven' and 'Piano Man.' Yeah. I know. Believe me, it sucks to peak with your first song."

He tossed his guitar pick onto the desk and went back around it to stare down at papers strewn across it that Arynne couldn't see until she got closer to the desk.

"Peak?" she questioned. "You've had countless number one hits."

"I know," he dismissed as if it were nothing. He started gathering the stacks of papers on the desk, his towel slipping from his shoulders until he finally dropped it on the leather office chair in disgust so he could finish his task.

Arynne stood fidgeting, trying to figure out what to say next since he didn't seem to want her apology. Then he lost his fumbled stack of papers as a bunch slipped from a manila envelope to flutter onto the ground by her feet. "What is all this?" she asked, bending down to gather it all up.

"The paperwork for this place: deed and everything. I originally came here so I could get it sorted out, but this is just impossible."

"Then why don't you just pass it off again?" Arynne asked, turning the pages she gathered in her hand until the words made sense. Then she realized that the ones in her hands were written in French.

"What? Bet it all in another high stakes card game?" He shook his head. "I'm not really much of a player. It was just a bit of fun, you know. A lark." He chuckled at his old timey phrasing. "Plus, I don't know. Look at this place. It seems a shame, doesn't it? For something that was supposed to be so beautiful and special to be thrown around like it's a broken-down trailer in a backwater trailer park."

Knowing what she did about Dion's past, at least from his Behind-the-Music biography, she realized Dion had grown up wild and free in a trailer park in the lake country of Minnesota, which frankly, was most of Minnesota.

Arynne gripped the pages as she wrestled with an odd feeling in her chest.

"Don't worry," Dion said quickly, running a hand through his hair, which caused him to lose more pages. "It's going to take ages, it turns out, to undo this legal mess regarding the house."

"But you will get rid of it one day, and then I'll be out of job, right?" Arynne said more than asked.

"I would never do that to you," he said as if shocked by what she was implying. Arynne regarded him, this sensual man wearing next to nothing with his damp hair. He had nearly everything she had wanted for herself, yet she could offer him nothing much in return. She wanted to move around that desk and run her fingers through his damp hair. She imagined the exciting, electric thrill of touching that well-made chest. A man's body. The strange feeling in her own chest burned hotter, and she recognized it at last. It was desire. A crisp fire that she hadn't felt since...

It was only then she remembered Thomas, horrified that she had completely forgotten about him. Again.

"I promise. Whatever ends up happening with this place, I will make sure you are taken care of," Dion continued, standing there in the lamp light, his chest glowing gold.

Arynne pressed her hands against her belly, even though it felt no different even after almost two months. They stayed that way for a long moment, neither daring to breathe.

At last, Dion broke the tension by shifting his feet. "Would you like some soup? It's ready, and it would only take a few minutes to warm it up."

"That would be nice. Thank you," Arynne said politely.

He nodded and replaced the towel over his shoulders. After they returned to the kitchen, he moved toward the spiral staircase. "I'm just going to go up and put a shirt on.

I'll be right back." Arynne's eyes followed him as he moved up the stairs. Once he was gone, she felt even more alone than she had before. And hungry.

Not waiting for him to return, she went ahead and turned on the flame for the soup. By the time he returned, the lid danced on top. She had taken a seat at the counter, back in the spot she had been when she had dropped off to sleep.

"Oh, sorry," she said, starting as he came in and grabbed the spoon left on the coaster designed for the purpose. "I got lost in thought."

He waved her back to sitting as he gave the soup a stir. "This is about ready," he reported and started ladling it into bowls. He filled both with a rich smelling broth and various chunks of vegetables of different colors. "This has chicken in it, so this should be easy enough on your stomach."

"Thank you," she said as he placed the bowl in front of her. She stopped his hand, meeting his eyes. "Truly. Thank you."

He cleared his throat. "You're welcome."

"And ... it's nice to meet you, Dion." She knew she was late in saying that, but she felt better for having said it.

He smiled again. "It's nice to meet you, Arynne."

He brought his bowl around the counter and sat down next to her.

"Now, can I ask you a question about that concert in Amsterdam?"

He groaned dramatically. "I'm never getting away from that night, am I?"

9

The next few days went by quickly. They ate together, meeting up in the kitchen at basically the same time. Dion had taken a room on the opposite side of the circular balcony from the master bedroom, though the term "master" seemed generous since every bedroom could have been called such. His had more of a view of the mainland, which mostly saw greenery and trees. He said he didn't mind, that he, in fact, preferred forests to oceans. Arynne didn't know how much to believe that.

Breakfasts started out pretty bland, often just oatmeal and the like, but it was all Arynne's stomach could handle. The nausea was definitely the worst. Dion didn't seem to mind. They cleaned when they felt like cleaning and explored when they felt like exploring. He was like the childhood friend she had always longed for, telling her stories and slowly but surely coaxing her to laugh and feel better.

With each swipe of grime, Arynne did feel better and better, like she could see a future in this mysterious, forgotten place. While the main building housed the essentials of living, with the kitchen, dining room, and bedrooms on the second floor, the secondary building seemed to house everything that a mansion needed to be a mansion. They found many interesting rooms. Other than the library, they discovered a ballroom connected to a banquet hall, a sunroom, and a conservatory that attached to the building with glass walls and roof. Many of the plants within had either died sad, dried-up deaths or had flourished into near jungle. Several of the glass panels were either cracked or completely fallen out, so Arynne decided that would be a project all on its own that could be dealt with later.

Outside of the house, there was a sprawling garden. At least that was what she called it, though the word didn't really encapsulate the cultivated jungle. Water pools all over spilled into each other until at last the water reached the ocean, pouring out in three different waterfalls. There was also a boat house that had everything in it except the boat that connected the house above to the ocean a story below. And all throughout were gazebos and at least three other guest houses, all in sorry states.

"This will take months, years even," Arynne noted as they shut up the farthest guest house.

"Maybe even eighteen years?" Dion asked, again making it sound like a joke.

She gave a small smile but found it hard to take it seriously. "We'll see," she said darkly and turned to walk down the stone path to the next mystery building. "This one is like the other two. Going to have to open it up, air out, wash everything."

"At least nothing has nested as far as I could smell," Dion commented. "We could hire more people if you would prefer? You don't have to do all this yourself."

"I think that would only be necessary if you plan on having other people here. Then yeah, I think I would need help."

Dion paused at a bend in the path to look out over at the view through a small break in the once cultivated foliage. The wind dashed around him, making his clothes, a strange combination of cargo shorts and a black and muti-colored pullover, dance around his statue-like body. The view looked out from their little inlet of land that showed a piece of the mainland. In the distance, a few boats could be seen dashing merrily over the waves. When the wind blew, Arynne thought she could hear laughter and joyful cries. Dion seemed to hear something else though, like some distant call he was ignoring or even hiding from. "I don't plan to have anyone out here if I can help it."

"Then I'll just take each house one at a time, as long as it takes," Arynne said simply and continued with her note jotting.

She could practically feel Dion's eyes bore into the back of her neck. She had decided to wear her sundress for their little tour of the grounds, and it had been a bad choice as the wind seemed intent on playing around with it, making the edge fly up.

"Dammit," she muttered as she batted it down at the same time losing her place on the clipboard she carried as the pages flapped like a bird trying to get free.

"You just don't seem very enthusiastic for all this," he said, though it felt like a question.

"I'm very grateful for the job," she amended as she got the pages under control and finished her note. "I will do as much as I can, but I will want someone to come out here and check the electrical and plumbing, too. That's outside of my abilities."

"Done. Whatever you need," he said. They walked side by side as the next building came into view. This one was closer to the edge of the story-high drop off. She paused at the smaller building. "I think this one might be a storage shed," she noted, leaning to try to look through the window by the small door, but it was too dirty to make out anything.

Then there was a sharp crack. Spinning toward the sound, her heart leapt into her chest as she saw Dion near the edge of the drop off. He seemed to be leaning forward, and she dashed, dropping her clipboard and keys to grab his arm. "What are you doing?!" she cried, yanking him back.

He hadn't been expecting her sudden intervention. Her momentum had him falling backward to drop onto his backside, his hands still thrust into the pockets of his cargo shorts. As he fell back, more bits of the safety fence intended to protect overlookers from plummeting off the edge fell away, the wood rotted, to splash into the water below.

She screeched again, stumbling back so that she landed on the man she had just rescued. He guffawed as she knocked the wind out of him.

In her chest, her heart pounded too hard as she pictured going over that edge and being crushed on the rocks below. Or her baby.

"Are you okay?" she remembered to ask, alarmed as the man she sat on started to cough breath back into himself. "Oh gods, I'm sorry. I thought... I thought you were going to go over."

"I'm fine. I'm fine," he repeated, waving at her while getting a good breath in. "I was just testing the fence."

Arynne's mouth dropped open as she looked back at the rotten wood. "That was dangerous!" Arynne shouted at the man who was now chuckling at himself beside her.

"What did I have to worry about?" he crowed. "I have you to save me."

"You scared me!" she shouted and whapped him on the arm repeatedly.

"I'm sorry. I'm sorry!" he giggled in between smaller coughs.

"I've never been so terrified in my life!" she exclaimed and stood up to go back for her clipboard, not because she wanted it, but because she needed a reason to get away from his laughing face.

"You better write down that we need someone to come up and install a new fence," he called after her.

"Obviously!" she countered and tried to write it down, but she pushed so hard on the pen it tore through the paper. "Dammit!" Her hands shook.

"Hey, hey, hey," Dion said, coming up to grab her arms before she scored through the board itself, but he was too late.

In all her rage and emotion, Arynne chucked the clipboard, throwing it so far that it bounced once on the edge then went over into the sea.

"DAMMIT!!" she screamed after it.

Dion stood there, his eyebrows to his hairline.

Arynne turned to kick at the turf, but she was already cooling down from her hulk-like temper. Taking a rough breath in, she ran her hands over her hair. "Dammit. Now I've lost all my notes."

"It's okay," Dion said.

"How?" she shouted, her attention refocusing on something. "How is it okay? How is any of this okay?!" she shouted again. Her voice sucked away out to sea. As quickly as she had filled with rage, she descended into tears. Her eyes filled up, and in her next breath, she was bawling. "What the hell?" she called out. "Why am I crying now?"

"Hey, it's okay. It's okay. It's just hormones, I think," Dion soothed, and she soon found herself in his arms, pressing her face into his shoulder.

Despite his comfort, she couldn't stop the sobs. They wracked her body. "I thought I was done with crying! I thought I had cried every tear imaginable. Dammit! I don't want... I don't want..."

"I know. It's okay," Dion continued trying, but this time his comfort reignited her anger. She pulled away from him and slapped her hands against his chest, not hard, but loud.

"No! It's not okay! I'm a terrible person. I'm a horrible, worthless, stupid person!"

"Why would you say—"

"Because I don't want this baby!" she screamed. The scream came out of her so suddenly, she felt like she was going to tear her voice. Every fiber of her being roared the truth she had been swallowing down for days ... weeks... how long had it been? An eternity?

Panting, she looked to him as the helpless man stood there, unsure what to do. Her eyes filled up again. "That's the truth. I'm a terrible person because I don't really want this baby or to be a mother. I don't want—"

"Of course, you don't," Dion said.

The stark statement flabbergasted Arynne so acutely she stopped crying. "What?" she asked stupidly, sniffing hard. She swiped the back of her hand, wiping it away.

"Of course, you don't want this," Dion repeated. "Any reasonable person would think that. You didn't ask for any of it, so why wouldn't you feel angry and... and sad about it?"

"But..." Arynne sniffed again, looking everywhere for the thought she kept trying to catch. "But I should love my baby. I'm going to be a mother, and mothers just love..."

"Yeah, and you will. But who said you can't also feel angry or sad about it?" Dion ran a hand through his hair. "Look, Arynne. You got left. That's not your fault, but it sucks. It's awful. Everything you're feeling is perfectly reasonable even if you *weren't* hopped up on hormones."

To go along with the sweeping emotional spin, Arynne laughed at that, then she heard the sound. "Oh, gods. I sound like a donkey," she said, which only made her laugh harder.

Dion grinned and waited as she rode the next emotional high. She had to reach out and grab his arm, she was laughing so hard. She sounded hysterical, which just made her laugh even harder. "I sound like I'm crazy!" she said.

Dion opened his arms again, and this time, she went into them herself. His strong arms around her body felt fortifying, like he could hold all her breaking pieces together if she just stayed put there and breathed. "You're going to be a great mother. You will. But right now, *right now*, the baby isn't here yet, so you can just be pissed off. It's allowed."

Arynne took in another shuddering breath. "How did you get to be so wise?"

"Therapy for some of it. Hard living for most," he said, and he laid his head against the top of her head and waited.

After a few more breaths, Arynne straightened to wipe her face. "Thank you."

"You okay now?"

She looked up at him, shaking her head but giving him a sad smile.

"Yeah, okay. I walked into that one," he agreed. "Look Arynne, everything is going to be fine. No matter what you choose, I'll be there for you. I promise."

She stood there with him, looking up into his earnest face, and despite her better judgement or what lessons she should have learned by then about the promises of men, she believed him. He continued to stare down at her with his warm, kind eyes.

"You know, when I first met you, I thought you were cold and..." She swallowed back what she was going to say.

"What? I was what?" he urged.

"Stuck up?" she said, wincing at her own choice of words. "I thought you were grossed out by me."

He pulled away then, shaking his head. "No, that wasn't it. I just... I have a bad habit of getting involved with people when I shouldn't. Ecstasy would be hitting me over the head right now if she knew."

"If she knew about me?" Arynne finished for him. "Who's Ecstasy?"

"My manager."

The mention of an employee reminded Arynne what she was supposed to be doing, and she picked up the ring of keys she had dropped when she went to make her rescue. It also occurred to her that she had been way too close to her *employer,* and though they were more like friends than anything, it was still inappropriate.

Did he think I was going to kiss him? she asked herself silently as she fingered through the keys.

"Uh, interesting name: Ecstasy," she said quickly, picking up the conversation again after a slightly too long hiccup.

"Well, she's an interesting woman. For sure. If it wasn't for her, I would just be a nobody playing in bars in Minnesota." He laid his hand against his chest. "Trust me, I have zero freaking ambition. I am only where I am because other people carried me there, and for that, I am eternally grateful."

He looked out again over the ocean view, his hair blowing in its wind. "What kind of life do you want, Arynne?" he asked.

She paused in her search at that. "I don't know," she admitted. The tenor of their conversations made her feel like only honesty could exist right now.

"It's what my mom asked me when we still lived in the trailer park. Right before all this happened. She was wise like that. I couldn't imagine a life like this one, standing in a place like this." He gestured at the ocean. "A world away from that dingy pit."

"What did you tell her? About the life you wanted?"

Dion grinned. "Fame, fortune, and all the women I could ever want."

Arynne cocked an eyebrow at him. "Well, you got all of that."

His cheeks reddened as he grinned at his feet. "Yeah, I did."

"Though I don't understand the women part," she said under her breath. "Why do men need countless numbers of women to throw themselves at them?"

"You're referring to the Bacchanalia, aren't you? I mean, my entourage." He leaned against the wall next to the door, sliding his hands back into his pockets.

"I did confess to being a fan," she replied.

"It's not what you think," he said, leaning in a bit more as if telling her a secret.

"What—that you have a group of women all throwing themselves at you any time of the day or night, never mind all the fans who would do the same without the special designation?" She sighed, hearing how harsh she sounded, especially toward someone who had helped her. "Look, it's not that I don't get you. It's the women I don't get. Why would they want to be one of several?"

Dion shook his head. "They don't define themselves by who they date," he said.

Arynne scoffed at that. "Bullshit."

"Says the woman who has been defining herself by the man who left her for the entirety I have known her," he said.

She narrowed her eyes at him.

He held his hands up in surrender. "They're not mine. I don't belong to any of them. And they don't belong to me," he stated. "Everyone is free to come and go. If anything, they are just part of the image. You know, Dionysus and his women. By their choice. We share company, and when they want, they move on. It's more about what they need than about me at all."

"What does that mean?"

"Well, for a lot of them, they get to travel the world. See and experience things they wouldn't otherwise. Some of them are back-up dancers, and they get access to other projects. Some get in-roads into various industries. One of the Bacchanalia was actually a doctor, and we did a whole project to raise funds for her to create clinics for refugee camps. You know, stuff like that."

"But you sleep with these women?" Arynne persisted. "You have ... relations with them."

"I have had sex with some of them, yes," Dion said plainly. "Not all, and it's not rigidly defined by that. We share companionship. That's all."

She scrunched up her nose. "I guess ... that is a perspective. Honestly, I always hated the Bacchanalia. It was the one part about you I didn't like."

"But it didn't turn you away entirely?" he asked.

She shook her head with a tired sigh. "No, no. Your songs were just too good. And gods know I've seen enough in my father's home..." Arynne stopped at that. She didn't want to bring her father up or get into any of the things she had seen in his house. "I get what men want. I suppose you're just more honorable. You're up front with everyone about it."

"Look, I'm just ... aromantic, okay?" he said, getting more defensive. "It's just how I am. I'm attracted to women." He shook his head. "I'm attracted to people, but I don't feel what everyone else seems to feel. I don't ... fall in love. I care about people, but I don't feel anything more than that."

Arynne sniffed at that statement, then picked out another key from the bunch that looked likely to open the door. "Well, that is why I'm never going to be one of your Bacchanalia. I don't really know what I want, but it isn't that."

He grinned and nodded. "Okay, I can accept that."

"Guess we'll just have to be friends then," she agreed.

"Yeah, guess so. And honestly, I like that," he said.

"Because I'm pregnant with another man's child?" she said it like it was a joke while showing him that she knew what he had to be thinking.

"Hey, Arynne," he said, setting a hand on her wrist to capture her attention away from wrestling with the lock. When she looked at him, he slipped his finger along her temple to clear her face from the fly-aways blocking her eyes from meeting his own. "The baby is your child. Not that bastard's. Any good man worth his shit would think that and only that. And if they don't, you just tell me, and I will beat them blind because nobody talks about my friends that way."

And she believed him. A feeling of peace came with that knowledge, and a grip like a tightened fist let go in her chest.

"Do you think Thomas..." She paused, wishing she hadn't started to say the thought out loud, but once started, she realized she couldn't stop it there, not with Dion's eyes so open before her. "Do you think that was why Thomas did what he did? What you said earlier. About being aromantic? He couldn't really love me, and it's not really his fault or anything? It's just the way he is made?"

Dion huffed a sigh. "I can't speak for *why* he did what he did. I just know *what* he did was use you for his own purposes, and *that* was bullshit," Dion said vehemently.

She smiled weakly in return. It was a small comfort, she guessed, but she would have to keep thinking on it. "Thank you, Dion. You are a good friend."

"Any time, my lady," he said softly.

Arynne finally found the correct key as it clicked in the lock. Together, they pushed the door open to reveal...

"A storage shed. Definitely a storage shed," Arynne noted as she took in the various dusty boxes and crates. There were even a few tubs of what looked like tropical-themed Christmas decorations.

"We should write it down... oh, wait," Dion said, looking back over his shoulder in the direction of the murdered clipboard in an obvious performance of teasing dismay.

"Oh, well. Too late to take the onions out of the soup now," Arynne said.

"Yeah," Dion said, chuckling.

"Well, we can't do much with this lot until I get another clipboard," Arynne said, pulling the door shut. "And thank you, by the way."

"For what?" he asked, completely oblivious.

"For..." She sighed, letting all her breath out. "For letting me completely lose it."

"Oh, believe me, I understand that more than anyone. I used to smash car windows when I was mad. Didn't solve anything and definitely got me a little jail time with a lot of community service. I'm just glad that you finally expressed it."

"What do you mean?"

"I don't mean anything by this, but you have been very ... closed off..." He gestured to his chest as he struggled for the right words. "Emotionally, I mean, the last couple of weeks.

Not really expressing much. Half the time I can't read your face, and I'm usually pretty good at knowing what people are thinking."

"Maybe I'm just trying to add to my mystery," she said. But even in jest, she knew that wasn't it. "I just can't feel very much anymore. Or at least I thought I couldn't."

"It's okay."

"I know. You said that already."

10

The cramping was so bad that Arynne didn't fully wake until she was bent forward against it. Whatever dream she had been having was wiped away. After an excruciating moment, her stomach relaxed, and she was left gasping, now fully awake. Dragging herself from bed, she went to the bathroom. And there in the dark, she saw spots of blood in the crotch of her sleeping shorts.

"Oh gods, oh gods, oh gods," she repeated over and over again. She knew what this could mean. Pulling hard on the toilet paper roll, tears broke from her eyes in wracking sobs that she then swallowed down.

"I have to stay calm," she ordered herself. "I have to stay—" Another cramp, not nearly as bad as the first, but alarmingly present, pulled at her lower abdomen. Something was wrong!

"No, no, no, no," she repeated over and over again, and she dared to stand up and leave the bathroom. Her long shirt covered to her mid-thighs. She couldn't make herself pull up the ruined shorts.

She needed help. Now.

As fast as she dared, she came around the balcony floor to the opposing door that led to where Dion slept. Outside the windows, dawn had painted colors on the ocean horizon, but she couldn't make herself appreciate the beauty.

"Dion, Dion!" she called as she knocked on the door.

"Yeah?" came a shout, but it wasn't from the other side of the door. Looking over the balcony, she saw him as he stepped out from the direction of the kitchen, his hair wet and hanging around his shoulders. He stood there in bathing trunks and a towel over one shoulder. He must have been early morning swimming.

"Dion, something's wrong," Arynne cried, fear and urgency cracking her voice. She cupped her hand over the tiny bump of her belly. Using her other hand, she pulled herself along the railing, again feeling a tiny cramp in her abdomen. "Something is very wrong."

"What's wrong?" Dion repeated, his voice now taking on the same urgency. He rushed to the black spiral stairs that led up to the second floor, coming up them just as she got to them herself from the top.

"Something's wrong with the baby. I— There was blood ... and I have cramps..." Her fear overrode her shyness about such topics.

Dion's eyes went wide as he came to the same conclusion she did. "Okay, we need to stay calm," he said and went back down the stairs with an alacrity that did not convey calmness. Helpless, Arynne followed.

"I think you need to take me to the ER or something," she said after him.

"Don't you have an OB/GYN or midwife or something?" he asked, not slowing as he got to the bottom of the steps, heading to the glass tunnel.

"Well, no ... no, I don't—"

"Why not?" Dion demanded, then swiped his hands in the air as if to wipe away the question. "Nevermind. Doesn't matter. It's fine. We can't fix that now."

"Dion, I need you to take me to the hospital!" she cried.

"I will... I will... Just..." He disappeared into the library.

"Dion," she pleaded, rushing through the door after him. "Do you think this is happening because of what I said?"

He looked up from where he stood at the desk. "No, I don't. This could be perfectly normal," he said, though he didn't sound like he believed it. His hands remained busy, moving around papers on his desk as he looked for something. A few seconds later, he lifted up a card, then grabbed the old-fashioned landline phone receiver from its cradle on the desk. The black coiled cord stretched as he punched in the number from the card, glancing at it twice before finishing.

"What are you doing?" Arynne asked.

He flashed the card at her, but she couldn't read it in the dim light. "I'm going to take care of this, Arynne," he said with serious urgency while dialing the phone base. Almost immediately, his head jerked as someone picked up on the end. "Hey, it's me... what do you mean, who? Your cousin... Eileen, I don't have times for games; we have an emergency here. Yes, the woman I was telling you about. She is having cramps, and she says there is some bleeding. Should I take her to the emergency room?"

He stopped and listened for a moment while Arynne wrestled with her panic. She was desperate for help from anywhere.

"Okay, okay, just hold on a minute." He pulled the receiver away an inch from his ear. "Are you still bleeding?"

Before she could answer, Arynne heard the voice on the other end calling out Dion's name. He replaced the phone to his ear. "Oh, is it heavy, I mean," he said, looking to Arynne without a hint of embarrassment or squirminess.

"Uh, no, just a few spots," Arynne said, then the phone started shouting again.

"Okay, hang on," Dion said then pulled on the spiral cord so he could extend the receiver to Arynne. "She wants to talk to you."

"Who is it?" Arynne half-whispered. She could feel her ears burning.

"My cousin... she's a midwife. I asked her to come because I wasn't sure if you had seen anyone yet. And I owed her a vacation to a tropical island—which is not relevant right now. Just." He gestured at the phone, now looking guilty as he gave her a half shrug. "I was going to bring it up, but I figured I could get Eileen here."

"You told your cousin about me?" Arynne cried in alarm. "What happened to not telling anyone where I was or *who* I was?"

Dion shot her an annoyed look as he tried to listen to both women shouting at him and failed. "Eileen... Eileen, hold on a moment. Just one moment! Please." He pressed his fingers against the receiver before his cousin had finished speaking. "I told her that you were a friend who got into tro—well, not trouble, but you know." He gestured at her when the politically correct word wouldn't come to him. "The way you are and could she come and help. I thought it would be safer than, you know, going to a doctor we don't know and trusting their Hippocratic oath."

Arynne hated to admit it, but she understood the logic of that. Her father had relied principally on family for *that* exact same reason. It just also meant Dion risking more of his family to help her if for some reason her father should find her again. Another small cramp pulled at her lower abdomen, lodging another spike of fear into her heart.

"What's going on?!" the phone shouted, the tiny voice clear if distant.

Dion pressed it once more to his ear. "I know you just got to the hotel, but I can come get you—" Then he stopped and listened. "Okay, that works, too." He paused again, listening, then held the receiver out to Arynne. "She wants to talk to you."

"Hello?" Arynne asked, pressing it to her ear. Dion gestured to the door, then left, but she had no idea where or why.

"Yes, hello. Is this Erin?" a gruff but warm woman's voice asked from the other end.

"Arynne. Yes, it's me," Arynne said, clutching the bulky receiver with both of her shaking hands.

"Hello, dear. This is Eileen. I just got to the hotel, and Zephyr is being an ass about getting me a car." The word "ass" was quieter as if she were directing that word away from the phone.

In the background, Arynne could hear a familiar clerk's own voice barking, "It will be here in three minutes. Just chill!"

"So, I'll be there soon," the voice of Eileen said, kinder and more directly into the phone. "While we're waiting, why don't you tell me what has happened?"

"I... I don't know..."

"I know, dear. This is a very awkward way to go about this, but everything is going to be alright, I promise. I am guessing from the panic in your voices that something has happened with your body that you weren't expecting."

"Uh huh," Arynne answered, her voice cracking with stress. "I... there's blood and cramping."

"Are you still having cramps?"

"Well, yes, but lightly. They were much stronger before," Arynne admitted.

"And nothing else has happened yet?"

"Nothing else like what?"

"More discharge?" the other voice offered as if it were the most natural thing to say in the world.

"Oh, uh." Arynne held still and focused on her body. "Well, no, I don't think so. There was just spotting."

"Okay, good. That's good," Eileen assured.

"Does that mean everything is okay?" Arynne asked, hopeful.

"Most likely, but I do not want to dismiss the possibility of something being wrong until I see you. Dion told me he didn't know if you currently have an OB doctor?"

"No," Arynne said truthfully. "I haven't known I was pregnant that long."

Quickly, Arynne took the receiver and set it to her ear as a stab of guilt cut through her. She *had* thought about it, that going to see a doctor was something she would need to do, but she kept putting it off, justifying that there was time. She hadn't been pregnant that long, but now, she regretted it.

Apparently, she *did* really want this baby.

"So, do you have any idea how many weeks you are?"

"Yes, eight."

"Is that when you had your last period?"

"That was when he left me," Arynne stated evenly. "We... we only slept together the once. And the partner I had before was a year ago."

"Or since?" The question surprised her, but why would it? She was living with this woman's cousin. Arynne was cognizant how that would look.

"Uh, no, no one since," she said softly.

There was a pause on the other end of the phone. "I understand," Eileen said, also matter of fact with no hint of judgement. Arynne felt grateful.

Dion returned. He had replaced his swim trunks with some inappropriate leather pants and a black t-shirt. He carried his boots and some black socks in one hand, sitting down in one of the reading chairs to put them on while his face asked a hundred questions.

"Should we go to the ER then?" Arynne asked, unable to answer them with her face.

"No, no. Don't do that. I'll be there in a few minutes. It is not uncommon for there to be cramping and spotting this early in the pregnancy, but you need to stay calm. The car is here! Okay, here we go. Do you need me to stay on or—"

"No, it's okay. Go ahead," Arynne assured and her new midwife was gone before she had finished the sentence. Instead, she lowered the receiver to the cradle. "She's on her way," she said softly. It felt strange to simply wait, but that was all there was to do. "Dammit," she whispered.

"Arynne, it's going to be alright—" he tried to say, but she cut him off.

"Don't you understand what you've done?"

"What—?" But she wouldn't let him get anything else out.

"You said no one else would know I was here, and then you go and tell your cousin ALL about me." She pressed more fingers into her forehead, compiled visions of her father and his men storming through the door and the sounds of screams. And yet, if she were honest with herself, a part of her wanted that. Wanted to go home, wanted the good daddy who would wrap his arms around her and make all the bad dreams go away, tell her she was the most beautiful and precious gift Heaven ever gave him.

"Do you want to eat something?" Dion asked. He had leaned his elbows on his knees once he had gotten his boots on, and now his leg was nervously jumping, like he wanted to literally run and haul his cousin to her himself like the roadrunner.

"No," she said softly, shaking her head. She noted he was stepping around her accusation, but really what more was there to be said? He had already told her cousin, and she had no other choices. So instead, she added, "Thank you."

It didn't calm his leg at all. "I need to do something for you. Please just tell me..." He stood up and started moving to the door only to boomerang back, degrading into a sort of animalistic pacing.

"Dion?" Arynne asked softly.

He snapped to her, going still but no less poised for action, like a knight waiting breathlessly for a quest.

"Can I have a hug?" she dared to ask, fear cracking her voice.

He crossed to her like a wave, crashing around as his arms swept her into himself. She held him back as strongly as he clung to her, and she could feel him shaking. They rocked together, becoming the whole world.

"It's okay. It's okay," Arynne whispered, comforting him as much as she was being comforted.

"I'm sorry. I'm sorry. I'm useless," he said into her shoulder. She tucked her own face into his, and they stayed that way for a long, long time.

11

"You're fine," Eileen declared, rolling the procured office chair away from the edge of the bed. Arynne brought her knees together to sit up on her bed from the awkward but necessary examination.

"Really?" she asked, relief pouring down her spine like cool water.

"Absolutely. Everything inside looks fine," the midwife assured. Dropping the speculum she had used to do the examination onto a towel on the floor, she stripped the latex gloves from her fingers.

When the woman had first arrived, Arynne hadn't known what to think. For one thing, it was impossible to get a read on her nationality at all. She had one of those faces that could have been from any culture with skin that could be described as well-tanned with dark eyes and dark hair threaded with silver that only seemed to give her dark tresses definition. She was certainly in middle age, but that range could be 30s to late 50s, yet the references she cited made Arynne feel like she could be even older than that. One thing had been very clear the minute Dion let her passed the front gates and over the threshold: She was in charge. In the same breath, she had introduced herself to Arynne and ordered Dion to grab the equipment she had pulled from her car.

He complied good-naturedly with a familiarity that made Arynne definitely believe they were related. Within minutes, Arynne found herself on her back in her master bedroom while the woman did an examination. After depositing her equipment, Dion had been chased outside, but Arynne could hear him fretting on the other side of the door, straining to listen in that everything was okay.

"Did you hear that?" Arynne called out to Dion, who opened the tiny crack of the door a little more open to hear.

"Everything *is* okay?" he asked to confirm.

"Yes, yes. It all looks like normal spotting," Eileen confirmed with reassuring confidence. "Very common early in pregnancy, especially based on the calendar you gave me. This would be the week of your normal period. We'll do an ultrasound, but I've done so many of these that I'm very confident that everything is fine."

"Oh, thank the gods," Dion sighed, sounding truly relieved through the door. Both women glanced at each other, then Eileen rolled her eyes as she picked up another black bag and brought it over to the side table. "He gets so emotional. Come up and sit against the headboard. Pile up a bunch of pillows. We'll do an ultrasound." She unzipped the bag. "And he can come in and watch this part if you want?"

Her eyes waited patiently for Arynne's consent.

"I'm sure this whole situation seems strange to you," Arynne said, getting herself comfortable against the headboard as instructed.

"It's not my policy to judge my mothers. If I have learned anything in my time, dear, ain't nothing happen that isn't a bit strange, and I've seen it all." She plugged a wand into her machine within the bag and started hunting around for the outlet it should go into.

"It's pretty amazing of you to come all the way here just to treat me."

"Oh, I wouldn't worry about it. I'm charging Dion a fortune for my little island vacation." She grinned as she lifted up a squeeze bottle that reminded Arynne of something one would use to apply mustard. "Now you raise your shirt, and let's take a look at your little one."

A sound akin to a puppy whine came from the door.

"Dion can see this part," Arynne consented. It was the least she could do for him.

"You are granted entry, milord," the midwife called, affecting a delightfully terrible cockney accent. It was so surprising, Arynne snorted.

Dion entered with gallantry, dramatically slapping the door open and gesturing like a Shakespeare player that had been spontaneously teleported off the stage into Arynne's bedroom at the height of dramatic monologue. "Forsooth, what commandest thou!?" he declared, though the pursing of worry in his eyebrows marred the comedic effect.

When Arynne chuckled, he relaxed, letting the persona melt away as he came around to the empty side of the bed.

"Are you alright?" he asked Arynne, though it was Eileen who answered.

"She's going to be fine. All normal."

Even though he had already been told, Dion's shoulders dropped a perceptible inch. For some reason, he didn't seem like he believed it until he looked at Arynne. Now he beamed.

A small sadness slipped into Arynne's heart. Would Thomas have made the same face? Grunting to herself, she pushed the feelings down. He wasn't here. He had chosen not to be here, and she didn't want to think about him anymore.

"We're going to look at your baby now," Arynne said, returning Dion's smile warmly. She was so glad *he* was there with her. What she needed right then was a friend, not a lover. She reached out a hand to him. His eyebrows shot up, as if her gesture surprised him, but then he took her hand, cradling it in his larger one.

Her attention snapped back to the midwife who squirted a large blob of blue transparent gel on her still fairly flat belly. With the other hand, she brandished a wand with a broad, rounded end. The cord went to the device she had set up on the end table and a dark screen came to life with gray lines and wobbles. A small speaker made "wah" sounds as an image resolved into more indiscernible blobs, but then the world stopped as the strange sounds coalesced into a perfect rhythm. Quick *wah-wah*, *wah-wah*, *wah-wah*s filled Arynne's whole world as she stared at a small spot on the screen blinking in and out of existence in time with the rhythm.

Beside her, Dion leaned over with a knee on the bed, his eyes laser-focused on the same spot.

"Huh," he said, bobbing his Adam's apple.

Eileen adjusted the wand against Arynne's stomach and indicated things with a pointer she detached from some velcro next to the screen. "There's the head, and those will be legs and little feet. Not a whole lot you can see just yet..." She marked the screen with the end of her pointer. Two digital lines appeared on either side of the tiny life and a row of numbers appeared beneath, calculating out a formula of some sort.

"Alright then, according to this, measuring the length of the fetus, that puts you at eight weeks, confirmed," she said sounding very pleased. "Just like you thought." She smiled

That made him look up, "Oh. Yeah. Sure. No problem," e said, then held the picture back out, albeit obviously reluctntly, to Arynne.

"Oh, okay," she said, now feeling wrong about kicking him ıt. "Um, what is it about?"

Eileen's eyes darted to Dion, then back, "It concerns althy sexual practices during your pregnancy."

"Oh, I—" Arynne said, her cheeks burning hot as she ınced with alarm and confusion at Dion. His own cheeks ent red, but instead of looking embarrassed, he grinned e a teenage boy. Or maybe that was what his embarrassed action was. Arynne wasn't sure. "Well... I don't know what ere is to talk about since I don't have..."

"I'll step out now," Dion assured her, "so you can talk to dirty old bird." He directed that last part to his cousin, o shot him a mock glare, which was completely undercut the laughing twinkle in her eyes.

"This is all perfectly normal and natural," she called k at him.

"And none of my business!" he called back as he disapred out the door.

"Dion!" Eileen shouted, just before the door shut.

His head popped back in. "What?!"

'Get me some tea," she commanded.

'Are you really volunteering me to make you tea after I paid for you to come all this way to a tropical island pare?" he challenged.

'No, I volun-told you to take your scrawny butt to the hen and make me some damn tea," Eileen stated, not at eterred.

Vithout missing a beat, Dion poked both of his cheeks in his index fingers, turning them in a mock imitation of an

at Arynne to assure her she meant nothing by her st
other than to confirm it, and Arynne took it that wa

"It's amazing," the soon-to-be mother said, looki
little image floating inside her. "It's like it's more r

Eileen smiled at her, then pressed a button on
of the machine and a little whirring sound buzzed
table as a black and white image printed out. Then
wife removed the wand so she could catch the pag
to Arynne. "And there is your baby's first picture,"

Arynne held the small image between her fing
icately as if it were the baby itself. "I can't even..
like she should tear up, but she was too filled with

Her baby. Her child.

Dion leaned in over her, craning his neck to lo
the picture, but she didn't mind. Instead, she he
him to look at as well, and he settled back to do

For her part, Eileen started packing up her
with a very satisfied look on her face. "Alright, now
dealt with the more pressing issues, do you hav
tions for me?"

"Um, not really. I mean..." Arynne blew o
feeling a bit at a loss. "I suppose I need eat a spe
take vitamins and stuff?"

Eileen nodded. "There are a few things to
and certainly it is best to be on supplements
baby's development. I've already got a list fo
over, but in reality, there are very few things
watch out for other than the obvious like alcol
Her eyes darted to Dion, who was still poring
natal picture. "There is something else I would
you about, but I think Dion should step back
for this."

innocent little child. "Yes, ma'am," he said in a comically high falsetto and then slammed the door so hard Arynne felt it.

Eileen shook her head. "That boy, I swear. A born comic just like his mother." She then regarded Arynne on the bed. "I do apologize. I tend to talk very straightforward about these sorts of things, but I don't want you to feel uncomfortable at all."

"No, it's alright," Arynne tried to assure, even though she *was* embarrassed. "I just want you to know, I am not with Dion. I don't intend to, you know, sleep with him."

"I understand, dear. And if something does happen between you two, that is none of my business, but I do need to do my due diligence in going over these practices with you, both for your health and the health of your baby."

"Well," Arynne considered. "I shouldn't be having ... sex at all while I'm pregnant, right?"

"And this is why we have this talk because there is a place for sex in pregnancy," the midwife said as she coiled up the power cord for her machine. "In fact, sex during most pregnancies is very good for you and the baby, and there is nothing I've seen today that would contraindicate that."

"Good?" Arynne cocked an eyebrow. This was the first she was hearing of any of this. "How... how so?"

"Medically, it helps strengthens the walls of your birth canal, helps with sleep, helps ease any pain and discomfort you may feel during your pregnancy, and can help speed up your postpartum recovery as well as decrease the likelihood of postpartum depression. It can also help move things along when it is time near the end, but that is not something you need to worry about for a while." Eileen reached into her bag and removed a blue folder that seemed filled with papers. She thumbed through them quickly, pulling out a couple of pages every so often to hand to Arynne. "Here is more information if you want more details, but I encourage you to consider it at your leisure, and you can ask me any questions you want. Believe me, I have heard them all."

Arynne stared down at the sheets of paper, skimming over the recopied type as it described things in a matter-of-fact language that in her father's household would have been considered so taboo as to even think such things. Instead of shame, mischievous delight flowed through Arynne as if she was drawing it up from the paper itself. Here was proof that such things were not inherently "bad" as she had been led to believe. A medical professional spoke of such things as natural and beneficial! What else had her father told her that simply wasn't true?

Still, her heart sank a little as she read off the other benefits listed that Eileen hadn't mentioned: "It's a safe partner-bonding experience."

"I don't have a partner," she said softly, before looking up from the page to the midwife.

"Yes, I know, but that is why God gave us batteries, dear," Eileen said with a grin.

12

Arynne hesitated just before the threshold of the nondescript building. “Are you sure they’re open?” she asked, eyeing the blackened windows of the unremarkable building. Only a single sign hung above it, *The Hetaera*, printed with plain letters and no iconic images.

“Yup, this is the place,” Dion said, unperturbed as he walked up to the black-covered glass doors and pulled one open for her. Despite the abandoned look of the outside of the building, the second the door opened, soft music flowed out of a colorful room within. From the threshold, Arynne could see a vibrant rainbow carpet that swirled like some sort of artistic impression of a spilling soda pop, punctuated with small collections of bubbles. Standing on the carpet were rows and rows of shelves covered with boxes and products just like any other store would. Unlike most other stores, small disco balls of various types and colors spun above, shooting off bits of glittery light as they turned.

Dion set a gentle hand on the middle of Arynne’s back, urging her in. She proceeded reluctantly, as if she expected someone or something to jump out at her at any moment and accuse her of impurity and scandal.

Instead, they were greeted by a tall woman with hair so high it looked like it brushed the ceiling. "Greetings," she said serenely, gesturing with two welcoming hands, even though a price scanner was held in one, "to *The Hetaera*. I am here to answer any and all questions should you have them. Feel free to browse."

"Oh, thank you," Arynne said, completely out of her depth and feeling it.

The woman smiled warmly. "First time in a shop like this?" she asked.

"Uh, yes," Arynne admitted, deciding to be a grown up and go with the truth.

The shopkeeper looked between her and Dion. "On your honeymoon?" she asked.

"Oh, no," Arynne started.

"Just helping a friend," Dion answered nonchalantly as if he took women to sex shops to buy vibrators all the time. Maybe he did?

"Oh, that's nice," the woman said, then took a better look at him, going still a little too long.

Arynne slid a sideways glance at Dion, wondering what he was doing that had garnered that reaction, but he hadn't done anything that she could see. His expression was in fact serene, like he was waiting and/or bracing for something. That's when Arynne realized, *She recognizes him.*

It had been a couple of weeks (was it really only weeks?) now since Arynne had made that discovery herself. She had completely forgotten that her silly, comforting friend was also a music icon of international renown. In her mind's eye, Arynne pictured the place being flooded by fans hearing the news and discovering them... discovering her in a store such as this! Tabloids and the pictures they would sport flashed through on the heels of that thought. Behind the shop clerk was a sign that read, "Discretion is our number one policy!" but that wasn't exactly enforceable, was it?

"Dion, if we need to—" Arynne started to say, reaching for his arm.

The clerk noted the move and then held up her hands. "I'm... I'm just going to say 'The Woman and the Moon' was a work of genius, and that's all," the shop clerk said, then did a single swipe of her hands in front of her face, flipping it from giddy with delight to disciplined professionalism. "Okay, I got that out, and now you are just a normal customer. Our discretion policy is one hundred percent in effect, and I promise sincerely that anything you buy here today will not leave these walls. You are just normal customers."

"Thank you very much. I appreciate that," Dion said in a neutral tone that sounded practiced and pleasantly distant to Arynne's ears. "Especially on behalf of my friend here. She's going through a really hard time, and it wouldn't be fair to her. You understand."

"Of course, of course. I completely understand." The clerk zipped her fingers across her lips.

"We're just going to look around, and we'll come to you if we have questions," Dion agreed, setting a hand on Arynne's shoulder to turn her toward the first aisle, which was along the wall and seemed to be filled with a ridiculously large selection of lubricants, lotions, and creams.

The shop clerk nodded and turned herself back to the price tagging she had been doing when they had originally walked in.

Once they were far enough away, Arynne leaned into her friend. "Do we need to go?" she asked softly. "It's okay."

"No, no, it'll be fine. We need to get these things for you. It'll be fine," he assured.

"But what if she calls someone?"

"Like who?" He cocked an amused eyebrow at her.

"I don't know," Arynne said, searching for what little she really knew. "The tabloids or something?"

"If that comes to pass, we'll deal with it, but I don't think she will," Dion said.

"But how can you be sure?"

"Well... I can't, but I have two choices to make in life, right? Let myself be overly worried about what other people are going to do or go about actually living my life and not concern myself. I choose not to concern myself. Now, let's get you some lubricants."

Arynne looked at the aisle, shaking her head. "I don't think I even know where to begin with all this."

He picked up a brochure that sat flat on one of the shelves, covered in colorful pictures of different kinds of lubricants, all with little paragraphs describing the virtues of the products. "Ah, start here." Dion leaned over her, using a finger to invisibly cross out a few of the images on the paper. "Eileen said to avoid anything that makes you cold or hot as that might irritate you at this time, but otherwise, the rest should be fine."

"How can you just do that?" Arynne asked, exasperated.

"What—avoid heating and cooling liquids? I've never been very partial to them myself; they're sort of a trendy thing right now."

"No! Talk so casually about it." She huffed out a frustrated breath and stepped away from him to cast her gaze over the myriad of colored bottles. "This is just no big deal for you."

The silence drew out between them, so much so that she had to look back at his waiting and frustratingly understanding gaze. Anger flashed hot inside her.

"Do you want me to go elsewhere?" he asked, not sarcastically like she expected, but with that gentle sincerity he had always shown her. "I can give you some space."

Tears beaded her eyes, and she brushed them away in frustration. "No, no," she said, sounding like a child to her own ears. "Just tell me what to pick. I don't want to read about it and compare. I don't want to study it. Just... just tell me what to pick and let's get on with it."

But he didn't move, only waited.

After another moment, she sighed and then took in another shuddering breath. "This wasn't what I wanted," she whispered, breathing the thoughts out loud. "I know. I know I've said it before. I've said it a hundred times, but this..." She gestured to the wall. "This wasn't what I wanted."

"You wanted a partner you could have sex with," Dion stated.

She growled in her throat. "Gods, do you have to say it like that? It sounds so vulgar," she snarled.

"Hey, no, no! There's nothing wrong with this. Arynne." He took her hands, her always cold hands, holding them within his warm ones. She couldn't lift her head to look at him. How did he always seem to strip her emotionally bare like this?

"I wanted Thomas," she admitted.

"I know," he whispered back, and she went to him, tucking herself into Dion's arms as if she had done it all her life.

"I don't want to feel this anymore," she said into his shoulder. "I don't want to bring him up every time—"

Dion sighed. "That's not what grief is," he said. After a moment, he continued. "Grief is like a box."

Somehow, the absurdity of that statement snapped Arynne's attention from the darkness she was sinking into. "What?"

"Imagine a box, and when grief is new, you have like a basketball inside the box, right? It hits the sides very easily and frequently when you pick up and carry the box. But then over time, the grief—the ball—gets smaller and smaller, and it hits the sides of the box less and less often until one day it's the size of a ball bearing, right? And every so often, it'll hit the sides again, but rarely, and it will make less of an impact, but it still will."

Arynne sniffed, feeling that allegory settle over her like a blanket as she understood it. "How do you come up with these ideas?" she asked.

"That one I can't take credit for. A friend told me that one," he said, and she straightened to rub at her eyes.

"I don't deserve *you* as a friend," she said.

"You deserve better than me as a friend, but unfortunately, I'm all you got," he said, plucking a bottle from the middle of the shelf to read the back.

"Oh well, that's very humble of you." Arynne laughed, feeling better.

"Here, why don't you start with this?" Dion offered, setting a bottle into her hands. "It's a sort of hybrid between silicone and water-based stuff, and I seem to remember I had a lover who really liked it."

He then turned and scanned the store while she stared at him.

"Your lover?" she started to say, then sucked it back. Of course, he had had lovers. Many lovers, in fact. She knew this, had read about several herself, and they even talked about it, but she still had a hard time reconciling this man with that man.

He didn't seem to notice though, as he pointed across the store. "Looks like they have dildos over there," he said, again so casually as if he were saying, "Looks like they have cantaloupes on sale." He moved toward where he had indicated, and Arynne automatically stepped along with him, holding the bottle of lube that he had handed her in both hands as if it were made of porcelain instead of plastic.

"Yeah, before her, I used the natural method," he continued, slipping his hands into his pockets.

Her head spun a moment before she realized he was still speaking about this "lover" of his. "The natural method?" she asked, realizing too late she had taken his bait when he grinned at her.

"Yeah, my mouth," he said, the twinkle in his eyes both endearing and infuriating. "I love using my mouth."

That introduced a different thought into Arynne's head. "So, is there something wrong with using ... this?" she asked, unable to call it what it was.

"No! No, absolutely not. Using more lubrication is always better," Dion amended. "That's what she taught me. And I've been careful about it ever since."

Arynne wrinkled her nose. "Maybe that's what's wrong with me."

"Wrong with you?"

"I've don't ... easily have an ... orgasm," she admitted, though her words got softer and softer as she confessed it. "I thought with Thomas it would be different, but even then, it was a struggle." Now she let the memory of their one and only time together slip back in, thinking about it now in a new light.

"Well... maybe. Everyone's body is different, and there is nothing wrong with covering all your bases," Dion said as he turned into the dildo row. Just like the lubricant row, there was a myriad of shapes, sizes, colors, and types all promising pleasures in big, exclaim-y type. On a first glance, she saw everything from glass phalluses to hot pink with ridges to a whole section that had a little rabbit with tickly ears turned toward the long, penis-like tips.

She couldn't help it; this row made her giggle.

"Ooh, my dear lord," she said out loud, and Dion giggled with her. The tentative ease between them had returned, and Arynne let her shoulders drop. It was as if they had been friends forever. It all felt so honest and innocent.

Arynne skimmed her eyes over the top row of boxes, all covered with pictures of various handsome men, each in suggestive poses. "What is this?" she asked, now amused as she recognized a couple of them as famous actors.

Then Dion froze next to her. "Oh, crap," he breathed.

"What is it?"

"No, don't look. Don't look! Oh gods," he said, then covered this face with his hand, his ears burning bright red.

"What is it?" Arynne asked, smiling big at this strange reaction from the usually confident man. She turned to where he had been looking.

"No, no, don't look!" he said, trying to hold his hand out over one of the boxes, but it was too late, and he knew it.

There he was, posed on the box, grinning his usual idiot grin. He had no shirt on, like the rest of the models, and a guitar in front of him covering everything else that needed covering, with one bare foot up on a stool.

"The Dionysus," Arynne read aloud, nodding her head. The laughter bubbled out of her, not so much because of the product, but because of the way Dion squirmed in its presence. It was just too funny. She looked back at the box and noticed the bright orange, star-cutout sticker on the corner. "And it's on sale, too!"

"It's one of our most popular products," the shop clerk defended, having come closer when they had started to howl in laughter to see what the commotion was about. "I have one at home!"

"Oh, don't say that!" Dion exclaimed and turned away to spin in a circle as if torn between running away and dying on the spot.

It just made Arynne laugh harder, big deep, belly guffaws that made her sides and face hurt. Dion gave up, letting his arms drop, then held them out a little, like a martyr seeking mercy. "Alright, alright, give it to me. I deserve it."

Arynne struggled to get a breath in and get ahold of herself. "So, what is this?" she asked, pointing to the celebrity row, not just his box.

"These are casts taken of different celebrity penises," the shop clerk filled in, taking down one of Dion's boxes and holding it out to Arynne.

She looked to Dion for permission. "Casts? Seriously?" She felt the giggles rising again but managed to hold them down.

"It was funny at the time!" Dion exclaimed.

"It's funny now," Arynne crowed, her control completely broken.

Dion looked to the shop clerk, shaking his head. "My manager told me not to do it, that I would come to regret it, and here we are. Once again, she was right."

"Oh, don't say that! I love mine so much!" the shop clerk said sincerely, completely oblivious to what it sounded like. "In fact!" Then she scurried away, disappearing into the backroom through a curtain of beads.

"Oh gods, my face hurts," Arynne cried, pressing her cooler hands into her hot cheeks. "What is she doing? Oh gods, is she bringing you her... your... her copy of your dildo to sign?"

"Yup. Yes, she is," he said, deadpan, as the shop clerk did in fact return with one of the dildo boxes featuring his penis in hand, the detached silicone member in the other. Much to their relief, she only asked him to sign the box.

Somehow, that relaxed Dion, and they started talking once more about various things while Arynne made a dildo selection. She chose a simple one made of hard plastic and silicone sporting a hot pink color and ridges since getting a simple straight up and down one just seemed sad somehow. She brought her purchase up to the counter, finally feeling relaxed about what she was doing. Dion's signing for the clerk had turned into a genuine conversation about music, and she waited contentedly for them to finish. Without missing a beat, the clerk scanned the items Arynne had chosen while she moved the box of Dion's imitation protuberance out of the way.

A wistful, naughty desire whispered through Arynne at the sight of the box. Some small, wicked part of her had wanted to choose Dion's product. But that would be weird, right? After all, it was a cast of his member, and that would be like having him inside her and... and...

Besides, it was too late. The shop clerk put everything into a black plastic bag with a cheeky winky face on the outside and handed everything over to Arynne while Dion passed her a credit card before Arynne could object. Everything after that seemed pretty normal.

As Dion led the way out the door, the shop clerk called out one more time to say, "Goodbye and thank you for coming in!"

Arynne turned back to wave politely, just in time to see the clerk point at the bag with a wink and her own mischievous grin.

She knew. Arynne knew without looking what it was, but she didn't dare confirm until she had gotten into the car, and Dion was backing out of the parking lot.

Underneath the normal, simple dildo was another box.

The one she had wanted all along.

"Everything okay?" Dion asked.

"Yeah, yeah, it's great. Thank you for this," Arynne added, closing the bag over her purchases ... and bonus gift.

13

"This is beautiful," Arynne declared as they pushed aside the overgrown vines to reveal the large gazebo beyond. Dion watched her as she entered the space, her eyes wide. She spun to look around. Her awe for discovering this place continued to amuse him. At first, when he had come to examine his prize, he hadn't thought much about the island estate. Its rabid decay had reminded Dion too much of the trailer park, the place where nice things were used and abused until they were rotten.

But she didn't see it with the same eyes. Instead, this place was a world of wonder that only needed to be discovered and restored. Even the grossest discoveries, like that nasty nest under the master suite's bed, had been cleared and washed away with a little bit of her effort, time, and patience.

"You know, if I'm honest, when we passed by this, I thought it was just some crazy overgrowth, like a tree or something drowning in vines," he said, continuing to hold back the vines to let in the light from the late afternoon sun.

"You didn't see the spire coming out of the top?" Arynne asked, gesturing up toward the top.

He leaned back but didn't see, just took her word that it was there. "I guess not. It's a wonderful discovery though."

She grinned at him, quite satisfied, and she turned once more to examine the room.

The gazebo was built of stone, very different than most of the structures on the estate. It was something more durable that could last in the weather. The vines had completely engulfed it, filling in what would have been open spaces between the columns with greenery. In the middle stood an abandoned bed.

"It's like a bedroom," Arynne exclaimed in wonder as she approached it to lift the mattress up. It was still made up but was covered in fallen leaves and bits of vine, which slid off to the stone ground as she lifted. "Looks like rope," she said, gesturing with her head to underneath. "It's tied to a wood frame. And the mattress..." she leaned forward to sniff it, "it doesn't seem like it's mildewy or anything?"

"Waterproof mattress. Insanely expensive, but effective. I slept on something like that before when I was on tour in Eastern Europe. They are gel inside so pretty comfortable," he said. He waited for her to react to what he said, but to his relief, she continued to be unimpressed with his life. Too often when he had entertained different lovers, all they ever wanted to talk about was his glamorous life as a rock star. They always seemed to be advertising to be Mrs. Dion Brewer without actually wanting to be *with him*.

She wasn't like that. She had been impressed by him when she had first found out who he really was, but after that, it was no different than it had been before. And even then, *she* had been more worried that *he'd* be upset that she didn't recognize him right away.

"We'll have to strip the sheets and remake the bed, but I guess this could be a considered another guest room," she said. She dug in her pocket and pulled out a small LED flashlight.

As soon as she clicked it on, he let the vines go, entering the room with her. He studied her form, a shadow now with the flashlight before her as she skimmed over the vines in the space.

For one insane moment, he thought about crossing over, turning her around and enveloping her mouth with his. Just the thought of it sent fire through him straight to his groin.

"It's too dark in here to really see," she said, a bit disgusted.

"Here," he said, now daring to cross to her. Instead of fulfilling his fantasy, he took the flashlight from her fingers and yanked on the poor thing's neck. For a second, he thought he had broken it, but it pulled apart, popping open into a tiny lamp.

"Wow," she said, amused by the small contraption. "It's so cute."

You're so cute, he thought but swallowed the words. He was smitten with her, but he couldn't impose that on her. She already had to deal with so much and had made it clear she wasn't looking for another mess of a man to deal with. He could admire her, but he couldn't give her what she truly needed and deserved.

To get away from the feelings boiling inside, he set the tiny lantern on the ground and spun himself in the air to land dramatically on the bed. For a brief heartbeat, he thought he would go through, but he bounced and settled as the bed creaked a protest. As if that was exactly what he had expected would happen, he made a very satisfied *ahhh* sound and slid his hands under his head.

"You going to take a nap now?" Arynne asked wryly. In his periphery, he saw her set a hand to her hip, cocking it sassily.

Too late, he realized that lying down on a bed with her in the room had been a dumb idea. He forced his attention up the ceiling.

"Oh, cool," he said, peering into the darkness there.

"What?" Arynne followed his gaze, leaning over so she could crane to look up. "I don't see anything."

"I think..." Dion reached back over to retrieve the little lamp to switch it back to flashlight mode and directed the beam up onto the ceiling. "There, look!"

As he swept the light across, dark stars popped out in the light, carved into the underside of the gazebo with thin black lines connecting between them.

"They are constellations!" Arynne said, sitting down now beside Dion so she could see better. Totally natural and innocent—with no artifice of seduction or intention—which just made the action hotter to him. He wanted to reach over and pull her down underneath him. He wanted her to throw her arms around his neck and let him devour her mouth. He wanted to lift her over-sized button-up shirt, tied at the bottom to show off a tantalizing bit of her navel, which was already bowing out with its treasure, so he could bury his face against her soft skin. He wanted—

"Orion, Cassiopeia, Canis Major, Ursa Minor," she said, breaking up his racing thoughts.

"You know your stars," Dion remarked, his throat raw as he shifted onto his elbows. While her gaze was fixed on the stars above, he discreetly reached down and adjusted his erection, so it didn't press so painfully against the inside of his pants.

She shrugged and then did the worst thing imaginable. She laid herself down more comfortably beside him. Again, completely innocent and trusting. Gods, he was not worthy of that trust. "When you're a lonely kid who's only allowed to study and read books, you learn things."

That declaration cooled his racing blood. Suddenly, he could see it, the small girl she had once been curled up as the woman lying beside him. Her sad gaze told him so much more than her words could about a pain and loneliness that he recognized. And if he were her, he wouldn't want to be reminded of it, and it wasn't his place to ask for more, no matter how much he wanted to know more. So, he asked a safer question. "You studied the stars?"

She shook her head. "No, not exactly. I studied the myths behind the stars. You know, the stories?" She gestured at the ceiling. "I really only remember the names of those four. I would need my book to check the rest."

A small strand of hair crossed her face, and he brushed it away just as she started to wrinkle her nose at the tickle. The tender gesture caught her attention and those large, beautiful eyes blinked at him. He knew what other men saw when they looked at her. Her features and attributes were naturally sensual, lovely, and exotic. If he hadn't known how truly young and innocent she was, he would have thought her an artful seductress.

"What about you?" she asked, jarring him again from his dirty thoughts, ones where he imagined cupping her face while she kissed him, then sucked his thumb into her mouth.

"Sorry?" he said, wondering if she would get suspicious if he just casually punched himself in the balls. Instead, he rolled over and transformed the flashlight back into the tiny lantern before setting it back on the ground.

"You really like constellations?" she asked, gesturing to the ceiling.

There was the splash of cold water he had been looking for. "I never really liked school, at least not for the learning part. I liked the people though."

"I believe that," she agreed. "You seem really good with people."

He barked a dry laugh. "I mean, I guess." He shrugged and lay back down.

"No, really," Arynne said, turning on her side so she could look at him, propping her head up on her hand. "The way you handled the shop clerk the other day."

"Yeah, that happens a lot," he said. "You have to just get used to it." He smiled, but then Arynne touched the side of his cheek as if to rub away the mask that it really was. His whole body went still at her touch.

Did she know what she was doing to him?

If she wanted it, if she wanted *him*, he would give himself to her and more. Whatever she asked.

Instead, he cleared his throat. "I don't belong to anybody, so now, I belong to everybody."

"Dion." His name on her lips made him shudder, and he seized her hand, pressing it harder into his cheek. She was stripping him bare with a mere word, and he loved it.

"Thank you," she said softly.

"For what?"

"For all of this. I am really grateful for what you've done for me here. For helping me after everything that happened. You didn't have to, and it was a big risk—for both of us." She leaned back, taking her hand away to pillow under her head. He wanted to follow, to push what he had been thinking on her, to get a clear invitation or rejection, but he stayed where he was. "I mean, for all you knew, I could have been crazy," she added.

"I knew you weren't."

"Really? Because it was pretty crazy, right, to leave my home and family to run away with a man on a mere promise." She put her head back down, tucking it into the crook of her elbow even more.

"I think it was incredibly brave," he said truthfully. "You took charge of your life and just because it didn't pan out the way you hoped, that's not your fault. That's just what happens."

"But I was wrong about him."

"Yeah, but he really didn't want you to know that. He's the one who lied to you. All you did was give him your love, and he didn't deserve it. That is on him—not you." Hearing his own words finally cooled his own ardor. He couldn't do that to her, couldn't make love to her only to leave her, not after everything she had been through.

And he was going to leave her.

"Hey, there is something I keep forgetting to bring up with you. Now's as good a time as any." He forced himself to sit up, throwing his legs off the bed. But when he moved to stand, he kicked the lantern over, making the light skitter and dance across the gazebo space. "Dammit."

"What is it?" Arynne asked.

"I have a concert I have to go to. I need to fly out tomorrow actually, so you'll be here on your own now."

"Oh, okay," she said simply, like it was no big deal, but there was an undercurrent of tension that he had become familiar with.

"Do you want to come with me?" he asked to his own surprise.

She didn't answer him right away, and he couldn't make out her face in the new dark, so he fumbled among the vines to recover the lantern. He wished more than anything he could take his words back. At last, he caught the damn thing.

It had almost made it through the barrier of vines into the actual daylight. And still she hadn't answered him.

"It's okay if you don't. It's just a hospital concert, you know, for sick kids, which might be upsetting, I know, but they're great kids, and it does a lot to help raise money for them and stuff. It would just be for a couple days; we'd fly out and come back. I would cover everything. Or actually I would just fly out and come back, so it might not be worth it for you to come with me."

Still, she hadn't answered him. He held up the small lantern to see her sitting on the bed, her arms wrapped around her knees, staring at the vine wall.

"It's alright if you don't want to," he assured. "It was just an idea I had."

"I can't..."

His heart skipped a beat, and he felt his shoulders droop before he could hide it. "Yeah, that's okay. No problem," he said cheerfully. "Just an idea."

"I'm sorry, Dion," she tried to say, but he wasn't going to let her.

"No, please, don't worry about it. It's no big deal."

But the mood between them had been broken. All he wanted then was to get away from her and give her space.

"I need to go pack," he said. *Smooth. Real smooth, dumbass,* he thought.

"Yeah, of course," Arynne said, and she got up and left the gazebo. He followed, and they walked quietly back up to the house and didn't say much else to each other until he had to leave.

14

Lying in her bed, Arynne released an unsteady breath. Slowly, she brought her hand up to her own face, cupping her own cheek as she closed her eyes. Then slipping the hand down, she caressed it over the cascade of her breasts through her nightshirt. The tips of her fingers danced over her erect nipples, and she gasped. Her stomach tightened in response to what she was doing, and she flattened her hand over the cloth, drawing the edge of her shirt up.

She was back in the rear garden, leaning on the railing of the terrace. Large braziers were burning dramatically, throwing all kinds of dancing light over the lawn below. Her father's guests were all clustered about in light-colored clothing, trying to look tropical and moneyed at the same time.

She was bored of them all, but there was no way she would be excused to go hide in her room. Her father had insisted she attend his soiree as his arm candy, and if she was being honest, she did prefer it to him bringing in his latest girlfriend.

It was weird that they were the same age, but the girlfriend's worldliness and frankly blatant sexuality made Arynne feel so much younger.

The fact that Arynne was here and not the girlfriend (Arynne refused to call her by her name) probably infuriated the bitch.

Arynne blew out a frustrated breath, letting go of the nipple she had been caressing. This wasn't going to work if she dwelled on unsexy things like her father's girlfriends. She closed her eyes again and fast forwarded her mind to the moment he arrived.

"You don't look like you're having much fun," a warm voice said as a flute of champagne floated into her vision.

Handsome men, and not handsome men, would always approach her at these things, but there was something different about his warm brown eyes and charming smile. He didn't hit on her like the others usually did. He seemed to just want to be her friend, and it was the sexiest thing he could have done. She focused on his eyes, the warm way they looked at her. How close he had been, the soft touch of his suit jacket against her bare arms as he leaned on the rail with her, his own flute of champagne floating next to hers. No ring on his finger. His smell was intoxicating, some sort of mix of cedar-based cologne and a musk all his own. Even then, it had made the place between her legs hot and wet.

Later that same night, she had found him alone in the garden, looking out over night water at the sliver of moon above. The space was dark among a cluster of trees, hiding them from the main house, and she wouldn't have seen him at all if he hadn't thrown something shiny out into the water. She came up beside him, but before she could say anything, he grabbed her. His tongue came into her mouth, sucking the air out of her as he pressed her against a trunk.

Arynne moved her hand away from her breast, letting it drift lower down her stomach. She wore no underwear, so it was very simple to slip her fingers between her legs. She was greeted by her natural moisture, and she moaned at the sensations.

While she was pinned against the tree, he lifted the skirt of her dress, slipping a finger into her panties before she could squeal with alarm. Instead, she squealed with bliss, muffled against his mouth. It was exciting and dangerous.

Arynne moved her finger against herself, feeling for that pearl of pleasure. It leapt out to meet her finger, alive at her touch, and she moaned with herself in her memory. It had been the most sexually dangerous thing she had done to date, and now, she only wanted to recapture how it had made her feel.

Her mind skipped ahead to the last night she saw Thomas. The way he pinned her down on the bed and the feel of his girth within her. She reached for the dildo that she had laid next to her thigh on the bed and brought it around, inserting it in time with how she remembered his thrusts. Her voice called out again at the full feeling, the muscles within her gripping tight.

"Oh Thomas," she whispered as she worked the shaft within herself, pulling it in and out with the rhythm of her hips.

She wanted to remember. She wanted to forget.

Within herself, she could feel the rising tension building toward that crescendo. Could feel it coming.

If only he was here, she thought.

"No, no, no," she said as the rising tension snapped.

Thomas's face disintegrated in her mind as she struggled to remember it. Yes, she could remember his eyes were brown, but what shape had his nose been? What about his eyebrows or the color of his hair? Sometimes, she thought it was dark brown, and other times, she thought it sandier, but too much time had passed. She had no idea which one was correct.

Growling in her throat, she removed the dildo and had to resist the urge to fling it across the room. Ever since they had gotten it, she had failed to successfully use it, but that night she just felt like it would work. It had to. It was anguish inside.

"Dammit," she moaned.

Dion had been gone a long time. His original trip of two days had morphed into two weeks. He had called, of course, so she wasn't worried or something, but he had said that he would arrive that day, but late, and if it was late, he would stay at Zephyr's hotel. While she had been productive the whole time, it had been peaceful. Her morning sickness had passed, and her belly had started to expand, though she felt it more than saw it in the mirror. Eileen had visited her twice during the time to "check up on her," but Arynne was pretty sure it had been more to keep her company while the master of the house had been gone. Eileen had been pleasant to talk to, but they didn't really know each other that well yet, so loneliness was the more frequent visitor.

Arynne got out of bed and went to lean her forehead against the cooler glass of her windows, but it did nothing to touch the raucous fever within. "If I could just cum, then I could sleep," she said, then growled. "Or maybe I should just take a shower." She had heard that cold showers were supposed to do something for this feeling.

Her gaze landed on her nightstand, and another thought occurred to her. There was another option, but she knew there was only one place she wanted to use it. And if she was going to use it, she was going to make it special. Going to her dresser, she pulled out a sundress, white and covered in small tan moons and seashells. Taking off her nightshirt, she let the cool fabric slip over her body, covering her to mid-thigh. Her small bump pulled against the fabric. This would probably be the last time she could wear this particular dress, but she ignored it.

Who was here to see her anyway?

Changed, she went to the side table drawer and pulled out the bonus gift the shop clerk had given her. Dion's face smiled up at her from the box, and she paused to study it.

He would never want you like that, a small, mean voice inside said. She didn't plan to argue with it, but what it was saying was irrelevant. He had been clear about why he had helped her. And besides, her feelings for him were confused at best, but she knew what she needed right now, and maybe this ... this slight violation that he never had to know about would be the sort of thing to finally give her release.

She opened the box and pulled ... him out. The flesh-colored vinyl dropped into her hands, and she giggled a little while at the same time she was fascinated by how beautiful she found it. A ping of longing sounded through her, of genuinely missing her friend, and she clutched the item to her chest as her other hand dug out the lubricant to go with it. Armed, she turned to head down to the closest back door into the estate's back garden area, making her way to the gazebo bedroom.

Walking along the waterfall ponds, she triggered the lights within, and they clicked on blue and green, giving the place a fairy feel as she picked her way along the stone path. It wasn't until she had almost reached the vine-covered outer wall of the gazebo that she heard a sound that was different from the natural hum of the outdoors.

It was the sound of a grunt.

She froze in alarm. Her heart triple beat, filling her ears with pressure, and she skittered back from the gazebo wall.

The grunting continued.

What was it?

She thought about screaming but knew that if she alarmed whoever was inside, they could hurt her long before she could get back to the house and by extension the phone to call for help. She continued slowly backing away. Just when she had almost decided that she would make a run for it anyway, her foot bumped into something hard. Glancing down in alarm, she stopped again. In the dim light, she saw the outline of a familiar guitar case. Next to it was the duffle bag he had packed when he left.

"Dion," she whispered and looked up again at the gazebo.

It made sense. If he had come back and hadn't wanted to disturb her, he would know that the linens had been changed out here, and he could just spend the night in the gazebo. It was warm enough out, even with the slight breeze from the ocean, and the vines would block most of that.

The grunting continued, and she recognized his voice this time. It had to be Dion.

Now with a new sense of excitement, she crept forward. *I just need to confirm it is him*, she told herself. Quietly, she approached, her heart beating equally as fast as it had before even if it was for a different reason.

Gently, she pulled back the vines enough to make a crack to peer through.

While she half expected it to be dark inside, there were in fact two jar candles that she had brought out last week, both lit and casting warm yellow light throughout the space. He sat there on the edge of the bed, his bare back to her. The blanket she had brought out and made the bed with had been pulled down, and only sheets covered the mattress now.

Her breath caught in her throat as she took in his bare *everything*, all the way down to the crack of his butt, pressed into the clean sheets. He was slightly concaved forward and moving vigorously, his arm pumping on himself as he gasped with the effort.

Oh my gods! she thought, not daring to say it out loud. She had a passing thought that she should leave him to his privacy, but she couldn't make herself look away. She didn't want to.

Suddenly, he stood up.

She thought he had heard her, and she had no idea what she would say, but instead he took a few steps forward to lean one hand against one of the gazebo's pillars. He continued to pump himself, groaning even harder as he leaned.

Holy hell, it was hot. She had never watched a man do *that* to himself before, and while there was a small feeling of revulsion, there was a stronger feeling of hungry fascination. A tantalizing secret that she was stealing. She let the vines go, but they held their shape, still giving her a naughty view.

She couldn't stand it now. With trembling slowness, she skimmed her own fingers down her dress to slip them into her own secret place.

What am I doing?! This is vulgar and... and wrong...

It was heavenly.

Before she had grappled with her own ramifications of what she was doing, her own groan escaped her throat.

She slapped her free hand over her own mouth.

Unfortunately, that meant dropping her toys onto the ground, and they made a clatter on the stone.

"What the hell!" Dion startled, spinning naked to face the intrusion.

Arynne stood there, frozen, still hidden by the vines with no idea what to do now.

15

"Who's there?!" Dion shouted, understandably disturbed. He dropped to the ground quickly and picked up his abandoned clothing to hold over himself, even though it was far too late for that. She had seen everything.

She decided she needed to face the music. Splitting the vines apart farther, she guiltily stepped into the gazebo space.

"It's just me," she said meekly. "I'm sorry."

"Arynne!" he exclaimed and backed away a step, his gaze skimming around him like he wanted to escape. "What are you doing here?"

"I came down here to..." Her face couldn't have burned hotter. "I came down here because I couldn't sleep. I thought a change of scenery would help. What are *you* doing here?" She asked the question even though she had already figured out the answer. It was something to say.

"I... I didn't want to wake you up," he said. He couldn't meet her eye.

"I'm so sorry," Arynne said, meaning every word. "I'll go back up to the house now." She withdrew back through the vine wall.

"Arynne, wait," Dion said, and she did wait. She wanted to know what he would say.

She wanted a reason to stay.

She wanted...

He took longer than she expected to appear through the vines, but she saw why immediately as he was now wearing his jeans, though he had only barely managed to fasten the top button. In his haste, he kicked the box she had dropped, and it stopped him.

"What—?" he said, then bent to pick it up faster than she could.

"Oh, don't—" was all she got out.

The light from within the gazebo lit up the box enough to reveal *her* secret now. He stared at it, and for one horrid moment, she thought he was going to laugh. Then his eyes lifted to look at her face, and she couldn't read his expression at all.

"I wanted... I just needed..." What the hell should she say in a moment like this?

"It's okay," he said in that way that held no judgement. He held the box out to her.

She took it. "I haven't used it yet. I just thought that..."

A too long pause.

"You thought what?" Dion asked.

"I..." She looked up into his face, into his eyes that were only darkness with the light behind him. "I missed you," she confessed.

They held that gaze for a long time, then he cracked a smile at her. "I'm home."

She felt the urge to hug him but resisted it.

"Welcome home," she said as she smiled herself. She was genuinely happy that he was back. They stood there awkwardly, neither knowing what to say next in this situation.

"I guess I should go back to the house..." she said slowly, half turning, reluctant to go but unable to think of a reason to stay.

"Arynne, wait!" Dion said with too much urgency. His hand reached for her. They stopped that way, holding each other's hand, waiting for the other to make the next move. All Arynne could hear was her heartbeat in her ears.

"You know," Dion said, his voice husky and a little unsure, "if you... if you want the real thing, you only have to ask."

Something in her recoiled. "But what will that mean?" she asked softly, her focus on the box.

"It doesn't have to mean anything—if you don't want it to," he assured her, squeezing her hand firmly. "You are free to do whatever you want to. You can walk away, and it'll be fine ... or you could come in. What do you want?"

She raised her eyes to meet his desperate, hungry ones. "I want you."

"I want you, too," he said.

He was on her then, the way she needed him to be. His hands cupped her face and held it as he kissed her, first just the lips, then his tongue slipped into her mouth as she gasped with excitement.

Dion couldn't believe it, but he didn't question it. He never did.

Taking her mouth was only the beginning, and he pulled her through the vines as she wrapped her arms around his neck. He heard the distant thump of her toys falling to the ground, but neither of them cared. He would make her forget her plans entirely.

The backs of his legs encountered the bed sooner than he expected, and he dropped down, which tore his lips away from her. She didn't seem to mind, but came with him, her knees climbing up to straddle him with a boldness that made him feel more comfortable about what he was doing.

She wanted this, and he would oblige her.

This time *she* kissed him, grasping his head to hold him in place. Her tongue plunged into his mouth like a woman starving, and he supposed she was.

As she kissed him, his hands came up around her back, pulling her closer. Then he skimmed them down to help free the tops of her legs from the sundress that was just not obliging. He lifted it up enough for it to pool between them, then repositioned his hands to grab the bare skin of her butt. She arched against him then, breaking their kiss and thrusting her breasts forward into his face. He took the opportunity to bury between them, kissing through the fabric and enjoying the denial of more of her skin.

"Oh gods," she moaned as his lips and tongue discovered a hard nipple through the cloth. He continued to suck, wetting the fabric with abandon. Soon it wouldn't be enough. He wanted the dress off.

He brought his hands back down to the hem and lifted, but the dress itself fit her snugly around her body. That was when he realized her belly had more of a bump than when he had seen her two weeks prior.

She seemed to realize it at the same time. Her hands dropped down to cover it, her gaze looking away and that familiar look of shame returning.

He didn't want that. God, she had no idea how beautiful she was.

Using his strength, he partly stood with her on him, in order to pivot so he could spin her onto her back on the bed. She squealed with surprise, and he lifted up her sundress higher before she could stop him. With access to her beautiful skin underneath, he set his face to her stomach and proceeded to kiss it with the adulation of a penitent before an angel.

She braced her hands on his shoulders but didn't push him away. He continued to cover her stomach with kisses, moving ever downward until he reached the line of her nether hair.

"God, this is beautiful," he said, brushing his fingers through her curls.

"What?" she asked, breathlessly, lifting her head dreamily to look at him.

He only hesitated a moment, then decided that if they were to do this, she needed to know the truth of him. "The other women I've been with, most of them are shaved down here," he said simply. He knew she could recoil from him saying that he had been with other women, but if she was going to, then better to do so now before things got too far.

Concern pinched her eyebrows, and she rose up on her elbows. He could feel her start to pull away, but he tightened his arms, asking her to stay. "Is there something wrong with—" she started to ask.

"No!" he said quickly, then added more gently. "No, I like it. I like you. You're natural and womanly. And desirable." He brought his face down to kiss her thatch of hair, never breaking eye contact with her as he did it. The pinch between her eyebrows didn't dissipate, but she didn't say anything more.

He thought about continuing on, going lower and deeper, to try to wipe that look from her, but he knew that wouldn't really solve the issue. Instead, he rested his cheek on her thigh. "I'm not trying to make you feel ashamed of your body. Just the opposite. I'm just being really clumsy about it, and I'm sorry."

The stiffness in her face relaxed, even if the pinch in her eyebrows didn't. "It isn't that," she admitted.

"Then tell me," he said, lifting himself up and away. She may not have rescinded consent, but she had expressed doubt, and he wasn't going to continue to pursue sex, no matter how much his body demanded it. Not until she felt safe again.

"It's not..." She looked away, her cheeks burning, her shame face so familiar to him that he felt angry at the men who had come before him and forced her to doubt herself like this. If he could beat the living shit out of them, he would gladly have done so.

"You can tell me anything," he insisted instead, gently, pushing thoughts of violence aside. This was about her, not them.

"It's just..." She blew out a resigned sigh and looked back to him. "It's just the last time... the only time... I was with Thomas, he did that."

Thomas.

He hadn't cared too much about the man. Before he had just been a fact, an idea, someone contemptible and unworthy of this beautiful woman. He kept forgetting that he was someone to *her*. Someone real and harmful and ever present in her memory.

"What did he do?" Dion asked softly.

"What you're doing now. He went ... down on me ... like that and I..."

Her legs twitched to come together, and Dion lifted up to allow it. She curled over onto her side, her hands covering her face. "I'm sorry. I'm ruining it," she said, her voice trembling near tears.

"Arynne," he said, gently, setting a hand on her hip. "May I hold you?"

She nodded, even with her hands still pressed into her face. He laid himself down behind her, gently drawing her close against his chest. She tucked in so naturally, warmth struck through him like lightning, and he wanted to crush her closer, as if his arms could shield her from all the pain and harm she had gone through. For a brief moment, he was struck by a memory he had thought he had forgotten. When he had been a teenager and his mother had been lying on her bed crying, alone and sad. He had held her too then, begging her not to cry and unable to fight his own tears as he tried to comfort her. He hadn't known then that she was dying from cancer. She couldn't bring herself to tell him.

"I'm sorry. I'm sorry. I'm sorry," Arynne said into his chest, breaking up the bad memories that threatened to pull him away from this very real moment. She repeated it over and over again like a mantra.

"Hushhhhhhhh," he whispered back. "You have nothing to be sorry for."

"I don't know how to do this," she exclaimed, not comforted by his words. "I want to. I do. I just—"

"If you want me, kiss me," Dion said.

She stopped fighting herself, instead looking up at him with her large, dark eyes.

He nodded. "Kiss me if it's what you want. Touch me. Do whatever you want with my body. I'm yours. Do with me what you will. Nothing you do will be wrong."

She lifted her fingers and caressed the sides of his face, tracing pleasure down the line of it. Then emboldened, she pulled him down, not to kiss his lips, but to press her own against his neck.

The shudders down his back went all the way to his toes, and he gripped her tight. "Arynne," he huffed out, though it barely sounded like her name to him.

She pushed him back, coming up to straddle his hips while he gasped beneath her. Her fingertips rested lightly on his bare chest as her gaze took him in, washing across his skin. His own hands naturally found their way to her knees as he waited for her next decision.

Then she made it, reaching down to lift up the hem of her dress, fully divesting herself of the beautiful but unnecessary pattern. Her skin glowed in the candlelight as he took the curves of her in. He had never seen any woman so beautiful in his life, his goddess. But it wasn't her beauty that drew him in; it was her. Her warmth, her strength, her determination. Only a few moments before, she had been afraid and ashamed, in tears, but here she was a glorious and confident creature. She set aside her pain to reach out for something more.

Her hands stroked down his chest, and he arched against them as she explored the planes of him.

"Take me," he begged, barely uttering the words.

Her fingers didn't stop at his stomach or belt line. Instead, she settled back farther on his legs and seized the small button, the only thing holding his jeans on. His arms were spread across the bed, a willing prisoner in invisible chains. With mischievous glints in her eyes, she slowly popped the button. A smile spread over her face as she peeled back the cloth to reveal his own skin, his own thatch of hair. Then she stopped just before the final reveal. He shook hard, so eager for her to complete the action, to set him free. He moaned as he rolled his head back.

"Are you alright?" she asked, genuinely concerned, which only made it worse.

"You're torturing me!" he declared, not yelling, but yelling.

She laughed as he panted before he chuckled, too, setting his head back again. "Gods, woman."

Then her fingers freed him, slipping around his tender flesh, grasping the stiffness, the painful stiffness, and giving him a tiny bit of relief at the touch. Then she bent herself over and kissed the tip. He groaned unabashedly, giving full voice to everything he felt and not holding any of it back. She slid off him, shimmying the pants down his legs while he panted like a dying fish.

"I can't believe I'm doing this," she said, not from fear this time, but with unbridled excitement. That was what he wanted to hear, what he wanted her to feel. She returned, boldly climbing up his body to resettle herself on his middle, but the second their most intimate parts touched, she froze again, all focus now there.

"Oh," she breathed, and automatically, her body gyrated a little bit against him. Their sweet wetness joined between them, and even this much sensation was enough. His own hips reacted with the same naturalness of hers, and he pressed himself against her, his hands finding their place on her hips. "Oh, Dion."

"Arynne," he answered.

This was enough.

It wasn't enough.

He wanted more.

He wanted this.

But he couldn't take it. It was against their rule. This was her journey, and all the moves were hers.

16

Arynne loved this.

She loved it all the way down to her toes.

Before when she had been with the handful of other men who tried to please her, they had all been determined to take charge, to "show her a good time." None of them had offered themselves to her, not like this.

Dion was so patient, waiting and open while *she* explored *him*. And this was the best. Rubbing her aching self against him, shot after shot of lightning went up into her core. It felt so good, but this wasn't enough. The ache was deeper, the desire hotter. She needed him inside her, and she knew it all the way to her DNA. Human beings were designed for this, and everything else she had been told was an awful, horrible lie.

"Arynne, please," he begged, his eyes closed as he writhed beneath her. She thought he would grab her and force her onto his cock—some small part of her wanted him to—but he resisted.

He waited.

He waited for her!

That in itself was the hottest thing she had ever known. She had control and power over this situation, and he would accept whatever she did.

Boldly, she reached down, touching his penis between her legs. It was hard and soft at the same time, the skin silky and wet, and she explored it with her fingers. While she had seen it before as vinyl, the real thing was far more in every respect, more so because it was connected to him. She lifted it up, pivoting the rod straight toward the gazebo ceiling. She knew this wasn't going to hurt since she had done such acts before, but a small ping of apprehension made her hesitate before she could flick it away.

Then he was in her, the head sliding into her entrance naturally as she lowered herself down. As he filled her, her breath gasped out. These sensations were new and long sought for, a feeling of fullness as he eased in with the help of gravity. "Oh gods," she exhaled.

"Arynne," he called to her, and his hand cupped her cheek. "My beautiful Arynne."

She kissed the palm of his hand, then followed her body's commands as she rocked against him. Rising up and down on her knees, she felt him go in and out, sending sensations of hot pleasure through her. They were doing it, they were mating, each moment getting better. She felt herself rising, felt the world fall away as she pumped herself on him.

She wanted this.

She needed it.

Higher she rose, and her own moans bellowed out of her with each thrust, lewd sounds that also rang musically to her ears. His voice joined hers, his deeper cries singing a harmony that she loved. She didn't look away from his face, a reflection of her own, and his passion made hers the sweeter.

Higher and higher; she would make it this time.

And yet as she almost crested, it faltered. The sensations were not enough. Her drive was failing.

"No," she cried out as she felt it start to fall apart.

Then his hand moved. He slid it down her thigh, and his thumb went against her clitoris. He pressed it firmly, and her world exploded. She not only rose but crashed through the invisible barrier. She called out as her body contracted around him, squeezing his dick hard, fulfilling her inside as mind-numbing pleasure coursed through her veins like lightning.

When it was over, she was left gasping, her body curling forward in exhaustion.

"That was..." she tried to say between breaths but couldn't as she landed on his chest. His arms came around her and held her close, one hand cupping the back of her head, the other wrapped around her middle. He was still inside her, she could feel his hardness pulsing, but she couldn't move anymore as late tremors continued to zip along her limbs.

"You didn't cum," she said, noting it.

"No, but you did," he said, sounding amused.

"I've never felt anything like that before," she breathed. "It was wonderful. I get now why everyone wants to do this."

"It was beautiful to watch," he said.

"Really?" She lifted her head, and he brushed back her hair to pinch the bottom of her chin.

"Oh, yes," he affirmed.

"But... but aren't you unsatisfied?"

"Terribly," he agreed with the same cheer.

"Oh, damn. I don't think I can..." Then her head collapsed back down onto his shoulder.

"That's alright. You don't have to." He kissed the top of her head through her hair.

"But I want to. I don't want you to feel ... unsatisfied."

There was a long moment, then he asked, "Would you let me take over then?"

"Yeah, sure," she agreed.

The arms around her head and body tightened, and she felt him contract underneath. Without her having to do anything, he spun her over, guiding her body onto the bed, all while remaining mostly inside her.

Now she laid back, cradled into the mattress, feeling warm and happy as this man hovered above her, supported on his arms. He bent forward one last time, to kiss the tip of her nose, then he was moving inside her. She thought for a moment that it was going to be too much, yet within seconds, she found herself moaning again. It wasn't like before. There was no mountain she needed to climb. It was simply waves and waves of pleasure lapping over her body as he thrust. All the while, his breath became more ragged and desperate. Grunts emerged from his throat, and he pumped and pumped. She threw her hands up over her head, her breasts bouncing in time with each thrust and rode smaller waves that curled her toes.

Then all at once, he thrust hard and froze, as if he was going to bury himself all the way to the core of her body. His head bucked as his eyes were forced closed, his mouth open in a silent scream. Then he drew in a hard breath, gasping for air, and like she had before, his whole body went limp, dropping down on her like he couldn't go on.

She *whuffed* a breath as he landed too hard.

"Oh! Sorry," he managed and readjusted himself to the side so she could take a new breath in. He tried to brace his head against his hand and catch his own breath. Sweat dripped from his forehead.

"Was that good?" she asked before she meant to.

He laughed dryly. "Good. That was ... indescribable. God, Arynne. Or rather Goddess Arynne." He set his head to the side, his warm gaze on her as he studied her face between breaths. "You are exquisite and wonderful and... and I would heap more compliments on you, but I can't put two thoughts together right now."

Between her legs, she could feel his member finally shrink and fall away from her, and she missed its presence a moment. As wonderful as she felt, she was a little regretful that it was over.

She turned toward him and tucked herself into his arms. Dion threw a leg over hers and hugged her close, planting another kiss on her forehead. "That was—"

"Shhhh," she said, lifting up her fingers to press them to his mouth. "You're done talking now. Let's just be."

He sighed, kissed her fingers, and when she lowered them, he kissed her forehead once more. "You're right. You're right. You're right."

Then his breathing slowed and deepened. Outside the gazebo, Arynne could hear the night creatures of their little world continuing to sing out their night songs, and farther off, the waves splashed against the side of their estate in a steady, eternal rhythm all its own.

Even though the night was warm and the man in her arms doubly so, she shivered all the same. Then he shifted, squishing her a bit, though she didn't mind, and pulled the bed's blanket back up and over them both.

Everything else was dreams.

17

Arynne thought she would feel regret the next morning for the previous night's activities, but she didn't. Birds were singing out as joyfully as her heart, and the ever-present rhythm of the ocean kept her asleep longer than she meant to. When she lifted her head, it was still dim in the vine-covered space, but sunlight peaked through a few cracks.

She remembered everything; in fact, she had been dreaming of their activities all through the night, and it left her warm and satisfied. She stretched an arm out, expecting to hit Dion lying next to her but encountered ... nothing.

A flitter of panic jolted her the rest of the way awake. Suddenly, she was back to that morning when she had awoken to find Thomas gone. She turned in bed, ready to run after him only to discover—

Dion still lay on his side next to her, one arm pillowing his head while the other slipped off from where it had been resting on her hip. He had been so much a part of her sleeping that she hadn't even felt his presence until it was absent. Quickly, her stuttering heart calmed as she pressed a hand into her chest. Suddenly, motion shook him, and he took a waking breath in before stretching himself. The muscles of his torso lengthened, and the sight of it helped calm her further as his eyes fluttered open.

He was physically different from Thomas...

Arynne closed her eyes, chiding herself. *No,* she thought firmly. *I don't want to do that anymore. I don't want to compare him. Not to ... that man. Not to anyone.*

She didn't know what this night with Dion meant, and she still wasn't sure how she felt about the man lying next to her, but she was done thinking of the other one.

"Good morning," he said sleepily, beaming up at her. He settled his arms behind his head, looking more delicious than he did last night. By contrast, Arynne tucked the blanket up over her shoulders and set herself down next to him.

"Morning," she repeated, pressing the bottom of the blanket to her lips.

"Oh, dear lord, you are adorable," he breathed.

"You're still here," she responded.

His smile dimmed a little as he took in what she said, and what it meant, before nodding. "I'm still here," he agreed. "And I'm a bit hungry?" he added, though it was more like a question than a statement, as if he were asking her if she was, too, and would want to go with him to find breakfast.

Which she did. She was ravenous.

"Well, I do have a fully stocked kitchen," she said.

"Good," he said and leaned forward to kiss her nose. "I'll go make you breakfast."

She giggled at the gesture.

He leaned out of bed, and her breath still caught at the sight of a naked him, even after everything they had done the night before. He didn't seem to mind, moving through the space with the innocence of the first man as he retrieved his jeans and slipped them on with no hint of underwear.

"Doesn't that..." Arynne started to ask but stopped herself.

"Doesn't what?" he predictably asked, turning to her as he buttoned the top.

"Well, without underwear, don't you risk, you know, hurting yourself?" she asked, gesturing at the spot in question.

He grinned as he pulled up the zipper. "Yes, but I like to live ... dangerously." He rumbled a jaguar-like growl from his throat.

Feeling like that was a challenge, Arynne let the blanket she had been covering herself drop, boldly pushing herself out of the warm safety of the bed. She felt so clearly naked as the cooler air kissed her skin, making it goose prickle, all while very conscious of his eyes on her as she searched the floor for her sundress.

"Dammit," she muttered when it did not make itself readily apparent.

"What's wrong?" Dion asked, finally snapping his eyes away to look at the ground where she was looking.

"I can't find my dress," she reported.

He grunted, and they proceeded to look together around the otherwise bare floor. "Do you know which way you threw it?" he asked.

"Well, no, not really. I wasn't exactly paying attention." Their eyes touched briefly as the reason why was passed unsaid between them before they both giggled.

"Ah, here it is!" Dion declared a second later, and he went to the edge of the gazebo floor and plucked out of the vines, seemingly by magic, her errant sundress.

She extended a hand to take it, but he gathered it up into his hands before popping it over her head like she was a child. Surprised, she gave a start before she realized he was waiting for her to put her arms through the straps, then he drew it down her form, helping it over the tightness of her middle, all the while gazing at her lovingly.

When the moment went on too long, he slipped his hand around hers. "Come on. The morning awaits."

The sun shone brightly through the overhanging trees, casting sharp shadows in elaborate leafy patterns. As they passed one of the many ponds, mist rose off its surface in smoky plumes. As they walked, Dion captured her fingers in his, and she blushed at the intimate gesture while he grinned as bright as the morning.

"I want to see you in water," he said abruptly before turning her with her hand, so she twirled dangerously close to the edge of the water.

"What?" she asked, deftly turning to avoid falling in.

"You're like a water nymph. I'd like to see you in your natural habitat," he said and lightly tugged her toward the water. She eyed it critically.

"We haven't even had a chance to clean these ponds or check the pH levels," she argued.

His shoulders slumped as he glanced over the questionable water. "I used to swim in all kinds of natural lakes without thinking about such things."

"Well, yeah, that may be so," Arynne said unsure, feeling like he was calling her out as a prissy princess. "I mean, I guess..."

"Yeah, then one of my friends got a bad staph infection from one of them, so yeah, you're probably right," he concluded and offered her his arm to lead her the rest of the way up to the house.

"You could take a shower though, if you want," she offered as consolation. It felt strange to hold his arm like that, like they were a dignified couple in fine clothing on a walk from another era instead of two young people wearing barely any clothing, and what they *were* wearing was definitely manufactured.

"I'd like that very much," Dion said, stepping forward an extra step to get the door for her as they reached the back terrace, his bare feet skipping over the pavement. He bowed gallantly as she approached, holding the door, and she giggled.

"Thank you, good sir," she responded, bobbing a quick curtsey before entering the cooler building. Everything was quiet inside. Just as she passed through, he came up behind her, wrapping his arms around her waist.

"Can I kiss your neck?" he asked softly into her hair, his lips barely an inch from her ear, sending shivers down her back.

She brought her hand up to his cheek. "Yes," she breathed and guided his head to the spot she wanted. More shivers and shocks spilled down her as his lips found the spot, adding his tongue to intensify the sensations. After the night before, she thought that she would be completely satiated, but even more fire burned inside.

Don't let this go to your head, she warned herself. *This isn't forever.* It couldn't be and she knew it. He had been very clear from the beginning about what kind of man he was, and she wasn't going to make the same mistake twice, falling for someone who couldn't love her back. But this felt so good, and it felt so freeing to embrace and enjoy it.

"I thought you wanted breakfast?" she said breathlessly, not pulling away as his mouth trailed down her shoulder, sliding back the material of her sundress to expose more skin.

He stopped and set his forehead on her shoulder. "Yes, yes, you're right," he agreed with a sigh. Then he stepped around her and headed to the kitchen. "What do you want?"

"You mean what can my stomach handle?" she asked, then gave herself an internal scan. "Actually, I feel a craving for French toast."

"Hallelujah. I know how to make that." Dion laughed and went straight to the fridge to pull out eggs and milk.

Arynne followed him into the kitchen, dancing around the space with him to pull down her ginger tea, just in case her stomach told her a lie and rebelled later. As he dug out the bread, she filled up the kettle, all while passing sweet glances at each other.

"So, is this what one would call an affair? Am I your lover now?" Arynne asked when the silly smiles got to be too much.

Dion shook his head. "I don't like that. It makes this sound like we're doing something wrong by someone, and we're not."

"A tryst then?"

He wrinkled his nose at that.

"Rendezvous? Assignation? Liaison?"

"Fun?" he offered.

It was Arynne's turn to wrinkle her nose, but she dropped her word game as her water quickly came to a boil, and his toast crackled as it fried. She retrieved the butter and syrup from the fridge, then pulled down plates, and by the time she had done that, the first toasts were hitting the plates. It was simple and normal and perfect. But while they ate, each perched on a stool at the counter, a contemplative look came over Dion's face, his gaze taking him far away.

"Hey, Dion," she whispered, her hand slipping out to touch the back of his. "Where are you?"

He blinked, coming back from the long distance, and flipped his hand to wrap around her fingers. "I am here," he said. He almost pulled away then to return to his plate and keep eating, but she didn't release him. She needed to know.

"You looked so sad," she said softly. She could feel him tense, and she shook his arm to release it. "Hey, don't do that. Don't pull away. It's all right. You can tell me."

Whatever resistance within he had left broke before her gentle words. "I was thinking of my mother," he said, his voice cracking. His eyebrows rose in surprise at his own reaction. Bubbles of water filled up his eyes, and this time, he did pull away to take his fork and cut another bite of the toast. "Mom and I, we used to make French toast like this all the time. It was something we shared." He forced a smile then, which only looked more painful for the shine in his eyes.

"You really miss her?" Arynne asked kindly.

He nodded. "Yeah. For all of my early life, it was just us, you know? Just us against the whole world. She was my whole world." He leaned back to tuck in his last bite, then stood to pick up his plate. "Are you done?" he asked, gesturing to her own empty plate.

"Oh! Yes," she said, surprised that she had already finished. She had no memory of eating it, just the lingering taste of real maple syrup in her mouth.

"Go on up and get your shower," Dion said. It felt like a dismissal, but she didn't want to leave him.

"Come with me," she said invitingly.

He took her hand, and she led him up to her room through to the bathroom. The shower was encased in a clear glass all on its own with a large waterfall shower head in the center. Turning the water on, she turned back to Dion who waited with his usual cocky smile. As she came closer, he bent forward to receive a kiss, but she stopped him with her fingers on his face. His eyebrows quirked together with a question.

Smiling, Arynne let her fingers drift down his neck to his shirt-covered chest. Slowly, she continued down until she could capture the edge of the shirt. "May I undress you?" she asked huskily.

"Yes," Dion whispered, and she pulled the shirt up over his head. As soon as it cleared, she went to his jeans, but he captured her hands. "Stop."

He held them for a long moment, his chest rising and falling quickly. "I'm sorry. I can't do this right now," he whispered, squeezing his eyes closed.

"It's alright," Arynne said. "We're not going to do anything but take a nice shower.

"I... I can't..." he said, pulling away.

She released him, letting him go, but he didn't leave.

He looked lost to her.

"Tell me about her," Arynne offered.

Dion's face screwed up into an ugly cry. Suddenly, he was moving too fast, tearing his pants down to step out of them before rushing into the shower and under the waterfall pouring down from above.

He couldn't breathe, and he didn't want to. The second he breathed, he knew he would be lost. There was nothing he could do to stop it. The pain in his chest flooded out of his mouth in ugly sobs. He had kept this held back so tight for so long, and now it came flooding out. And over something as stupid as French toast?! He leaned his hands against the wall, his body jerking with each sob like he was going to vomit.

When her hands touched his back, it finished him off. He spun around toward her, and she pulled him into her arms. He wrapped his own around her so tight, he thought he was crushing her, but she didn't protest and didn't try to get away.

"You're okay. You're okay," she kept saying over and over as she drew her hand over his soaked hair.

"I'm sorry. I'm sorry," he kept repeating. He had no clue how unsexy this was. He had never shown such raw emotion in front of any lover or friend he had ever had in his life. He didn't even know this lived within him, and yet it poured out with an acidic familiarity.

His legs buckled, and he dropped to the floor. She was unable to hold him, but she didn't completely let go. Instead, he found himself collapsed on his side, and she positioned herself so she held him across her lap in her arms. The water from the shower above bounced off their legs. They stayed that way for a long time, her rocking him gently with his arms wrapped around her waist, and his tears blended away with the shower water.

"She died," he finally said, sniffing hard. "Right before I made it big. She had cancer. Even if I had had the money I do now, they told me I couldn't have saved her."

"So, you make her live on in your music," Arynne said.

He turned his head to look up at her.

"'French Toast at Midnight.' That's about your mother, isn't it?" she asked, "The way, in the chorus, how the woman in the song keeps saying 'baby.' She wasn't talking to a boyfriend. She meant you. Her baby."

He nodded, closing his eyes as she snuggled him against her breast. "I didn't think anybody got it."

"I wouldn't have if I didn't know you," Arynne assured him.

"I mean, you can interpret it however you want. That's the point," he amended. "You know, the night I won the Grammy for that song, it felt like, just for a moment, that she was alive again."

The beautiful angel holding him smiled. "I saw your acceptance speech for that. It was very moving."

"But it didn't bring her back."

"It did. In its own way," she assured him.

"Thank you, Arynne."

"For what?" she asked.

"For not freaking out when I cried."

"You've seen my tears plenty of times," she said, then bent forward and kissed him gently on the lips. It was a light kiss, tender and sweet, with all the innocence of the Garden of Eden.

This is home, he thought.

18

"*J'aimerais parler à M. Carlier, s'il vous plaît,*[1]" Arynne said as she pinned the phone between her ear and her shoulder. All of the papers that Dion had were spread out in front of her, covering every inch of the dining room table. She had it sorted out into what she thought were various piles of cohesion, but she only spoke French and German of the languages currently represented. She had plans for using online translation systems to figure out the rest, especially the one written in some Asian language that she was pretty sure was not Chinese and that was as far as she had gotten on that.

What she did feel she had was a timeline, since all of the pages had the same number system for dates. So currently, she was starting at the beginning.

"*M. Carlier ne travaille pas ici,*"[2] the stiff female voice told her on the other end.

---

1 I would like to speak to Mr. Carlier, please.

2 Mr. Carlier does not work here.

"*Le formulaire que j'ai le répertorie comme personne ressource pour ce compte,*[3]" she said, reading off from the form.

"*Une seconde s'il vous plait. Pouvez-vous me donner votre numéro de compte?*[4]"

Arynne read it off, then waited.

"*Ce compte a été transféré à National German Bank.*[5]" That made Arynne's eyebrows rise. There were at least three stacks of German papers, each with different logos, so she knew where she needed to look next.

"*Avez-vous le numéro de contact de la personne à qui il a été transféré*[6]*?*"

"*Oui, madame. Un moment.*" Despite her terseness, the woman on the other end was very professional and thorough, giving her the original contact's name over at the National German Bank, but also who she knew had taken over that role two years prior and their contact information. Arynne thanked her and hung up, very pleased with herself.

"That was unbelievably sex—" Dion started to comment, then stopped and recalibrated. "Smarty. Yes. Smarty is what I meant to say." She glanced over her shoulder at him leaning against the entryway. He must have been standing there awhile because several plastic bags sat around his feet, and two long poles leaned against the wall next to him.

"What was?" she asked, grinning.

"Woman doing business in French. Objectively smarty." She knew that wasn't what he meant to say, and she was grateful for the shift.

---

[3] The form I have lists him as the point person for this account.

[4] One second please. Can you give me your account number?

[5] That account was transferred to National German Bank.

[6] Do you have the contact number for who it was transferred to?

"Only if I could say I'm making any real progress." She stapled the pages in her hand together and stuck them in a fresh manila folder.

Dion came the rest of the way into the room, bringing his cleaning supplies with him. When he got to the fountain, he looked inside one of the "cups."

"You got these all cleaned out," he noted, his foot tapping one of the garbage bags, now full of leaves and detritus, which sat next to it.

"Yeah, but then I tried to do this..." Arynne went over to the wall and flipped a switch in a row of switches that were the same color as the marble. Immediately, there was a *kathunk* sound followed by a grinding. The fountain itself made strange belching *gag* that produced no water.

"Oh, that's not good," Dion said.

"No, it is not," Arynne agreed and flipped the switch back to off, returning them to the peaceful paradise of silence.

Dion knelt down and flipped up the panel they had found a few days before, like everything, blended into the floor. It had taken a small turnkey they had found on his ring to make a handle to lift the marble-looking plate to reveal the water shut off valve near the fountain. Arynne joined him to look down into the square filled with pipes.

"Okay, well outside of turning the shut-off valve, this is now outside my abilities." He looked up at Arynne, propping his elbow on his bent knee. "I mean, you need me to install a toilet sure, but this...?"

"I can't even install a toilet," Arynne said, then noticed the twin poles he had set down beside them. "What are those?"

"Oh, check this out," he said, standing up with one of the poles. He pressed a button on the side like it was an umbrella. Two tines popped open at the top and locked automatically into a giant squeegee. "For the windows!" he said proudly.

Then he twisted the pole and extended it to twice its length. "We can reach all the way to the top."

She laughed. "You're very excited about this," Arynne noted. He popped hers open and held it out to her. She took it, but it was awkwardly balanced, so it took both her hands to hold it. "Well, I've already called a plumber. They'll be here later this afternoon."

"Oh," Dion said.

"Uh, I'm paying for it from the house accounts," Arynne assured.

"House accounts?" Dion curled an eyebrow at her.

"Yes, I found them." Now it was Arynne's turn to march proudly over to her table of papers. She picked up a small stack and flipped through quickly to find the sheet she wanted to show him. "I found this while sorting, and it turns out," she flipped it over to reveal where someone had written in sloppy print, "they wrote down the login and password, so I went ahead and logged in to the Island Bank system." She then pulled the laptop Dion had bought her, or bought the house rather, which had now been buried under another stack of papers. She cleared the screen to show him the bank she had logged into, but it had already timed out. "Oh crap, one second," she amended, passing him the pole quickly in order to retype in the password. "There, see!"

He leaned forward to look at the computer, close enough for her to get a whiff of his sweat soaked hair and body. Some part of her brain knew she should find the smell repugnant, but instead her toes curled, and she involuntarily swallowed.

Dion whistled. "Dear Lord, there's over a million dollars in there?"

"Yeah," she said, clearing her throat. "It looks like the original owners started this account sort of like a money market. What money that remains in the account has an interest rate. And since it's laid fallow for a long time, it did nothing but accumulate interest."

"Yeah, but a million?"

"It had a sizable chunk put in to start with," Arynne explained, setting the laptop down.

"You are amazing," he said after a moment, then popped up to plant a small kiss on her cheek. "Absolutely amazing."

"It's no big deal..." she tried to say. "Frankly, this could have been a whole lot more if they had put it in a basic CD or even just a mutual fund or something."

"Okay, I can see your mouth moving, and I know words are coming out, but I have no idea what any of that means," he said good-naturedly. "I am absolutely crap with money, so the fact that you understand all that is a miracle."

"I've always been good with numbers," she admitted, though it was embarrassing to do so. "My father... he saw a lot of value in it."

"That's a loaded statement," Dion noted, going back to the door for the rest of his cleaning supplies.

"I mean, it's not bad. It's not a bad thing to like numbers," she defended.

"I'm not trying to say it's a bad thing. I do believe I cited 'miracle,' but if you're only doing it because your father wanted you to..." He shrugged instead of finishing his thought. He also was no longer looking at her, his focus dark and far, far away.

"Hey," Arynne said, sharply, snapping his attention back. "Don't talk to me like that. I didn't do anything wrong."

Dion blew out a breath and shook his head. "I'm sorry. You're right."

Arynne let down her defenses again. "I know your relationship with your father isn't great."

Dion laughed dryly. "It's non-existent. Trust me. The rock legend, whose romantic exploits were as legendary as the man himself." Dion crossed to his bags of cleaning supplies and picked them up violently. "You have no idea what it is like to be one of several unrecognized children fathered by someone as selfish as him. And the only reason *he* recognizes me *now* is because I won a couple Grammy's. You don't want to hear about the first time I met him."

"I do," Arynne said following him with the two bags he left behind.

Dion dropped his shoulders as he dropped the bags on the counters. "I don't want to feel angry right now. I was having a really good day."

"Talking about him makes you angry?"

He smiled weakly. "It's one of my unresolved issues."

Arynne nodded. "Okay, it's fine," she assured. It had been their way for the last week, giving and taking, making love and talking, but always backing away when the other said stop. It was a rhythm of life Arynne enjoyed.

"So, here's my thinking," Dion interrupted as he leaned on one of the poles to cast his gaze over the windows. "The windows are going to take a while, and it's going to rain again today, so we can set these aside for now and go to the storage shed and actually inventory what is in there. What do you say?"

He turned his gaze back to her, eyes bright and excited for the adventure.

"You're like a little boy." Arynne laughed.

"Oh, hell yeah, this is fun." He beamed.

"Well, I'm not having fun!" a new voice interrupted.

###

Dion froze at the sound of the voice. For the first time in her life, Arynne saw a full frown bloom on his face, then his eyes closed as if in silent prayer.

Arynne stared at the woman leaning against the door. She looked like a nun had gone on a bender. The black, form-fitting catsuit went from the top of her neck to over the backs of her hands, looping through each finger and then down again into tall boots with hooker heels that could also be used as a murder weapon. Over her shoulders of the catsuit was a diamond-shaped hint of a white parka, which was what made Arynne think nun. It seemed to be made from the skin of some poor animal who didn't deserve that fate. The woman had a crest instead of hair, with one half shaved bald while the other side flowed an unnatural gray color all the way down to one shoulder. Dark-colored eyes similar to Arynne's own emerged from behind a pair of large sunglasses as she pulled them down to make her own assessment of Arynne.

The way the woman raked her up and down, Arynne knew how she looked in her last oversized shirt. Her pants were starting to not fit, so she was wearing a skirt that did not go at all, but both were comfortable, and she had been cleaning anyway.

"Do you know how damned long it is to even get to this stupid island?" the stranger said to Arynne, as if that was somehow her fault and she should take responsibility for it.

"Not hard enough, apparently," Dion commented, finally turning around and capturing the newcomer's attention. He crossed his arms, mirroring the intruder. "Arynne, this is my manager, Ecstasy," he said, gesturing with one hand. "Ecstasy, this is Arynne. Ecstasy is here to drag me back kicking and screaming."

"Well, someone has to. There is a lot of money, and my reputation on the line," Ecstasy said, finally coming in the rest of the way through the doorway, folding her eyeglasses up, then chucking them at the travel bag sitting by the door. "So, this is your current pet project? Or is this a mess I have to clean up?"

Dion took a step forward in front of Arynne, then held out his arms to the stranger, and after a cynical look down her nose at him, she softened a bit and stepped into his arms to give him a hug.

Arynne felt like a horse had kicked her in the stomach.

"Well, it's good to see you, and I am sorry about not calling you back last night," Dion said, releasing her by slapping both of her shoulders in a camaraderie clap along with an enormous sigh.

"That's fine, but let's go. Don't bother packing a bag. We'll buy you new clothes there. I've got a driver waiting outside, so as soon as you say your good-byes to this one," she indicated Arynne with a "wicked witch" wave of her hand, "then we can get the fuck out of this bug-filled paradise," she finished with a sickly-sweet tone.

"Ecstasy—"

"One week. You promised me you were going to disappear for one week, and I have covered for you, but play time is over. I'm just grateful I didn't show up here with you covered in white powder and a woman for every finger on your hands." She looked back at Arynne, again assessing her up and down and not finding a pasty anywhere. "Far more NDAs to get signed that way, and hey, who is this staring at me like a bitch?"

"Ecstasy, stop it," Dion warned. "Be nice. This is my friend, Arynne. I hired her to be the caretaker of this house while we sort it out."

All the words that Dion said were true, and each was still a knife through Arynne.

A calculation ran through the woman's eyes as she assessed Arynne again with that new information. "Okay, fine. Well, I'm here to get you, so if you can kindly march that way, I have a car waiting to take us." She pointed at the door as if she expected him to do exactly that right that second.

Dion glanced at Arynne, not saying anything. The tension in the room tightened. Another calculation seemed to burn through the manager, even though she hadn't moved a muscle. Suddenly, it broke, and she snapped a phone out like a hidden weapon, though Arynne had no freaking idea where she could possibly have been keeping it in that catsuit.

"Or you can*not*, if you want. I can just make a few phone calls, cancel the tour, and refund all those tickets. Pretty sure Ticketmaster will sue us over breach of contract without you being on life support, but it's not unprecedented. I think your father has done it a few times. Then we'll have to put together a press release explaining to all your fans why you're unavailable right now because you 'just don't feel it anymore.' We could do it as a video, you know, for that personal touch."

"Ecstasy..." Dion tried to interrupt, but she waved a hand in his face.

"No, no, no. I'll call Masters right now and have him start—Oh, my gods, do you get any damn signal out here?" She held up her phone in search of a signal.

Dion closed his hand over her phone, bringing it back down, closing it, and trapping her fingers around it as well. "Stop," he ordered, and she did. "I'll do the tour. Just give me a couple of minutes."

"Yeah, okay," Ecstasy answered, meekly this time, with a little candy girl voice. She backed away and tucked her phone away, again making it disappear like a parlor trick into some trans-dimensional pocket of her suit. She glanced at Arynne with a small triumphant smile, like she had won some contest that Arynne didn't know they were competing in. She hadn't even known this woman existed until five minutes ago, and this was all happening too fast.

She looked to Dion to clarify *what* was happening, but he only gazed at the floor, clearly unable to meet her eye. The sick feeling inside clenched harder as she put it all together. The dream bubble from the last week had popped. Hard.

"Can I grab my guitar?" Dion asked.

Ecstasy narrowed her eyes at him. "Fine," she said, sighing again in that valley girl voice. "I'll meet you out in the car."

He nodded and turned without saying anything to Arynne to head to the library that had been his de facto music studio, leaving the two women alone and with varying degrees of confusion.

"Now, little sweetie, you're going to need to tell me right now: are you fucking him?" Ecstasy asked with no preamble.

Arynne's mouth dropped open as she fumbled for a word, any word, to say in response.

Ecstasy waved a hand in the air as if swiping right to skip ahead. "Oh, great. You are. That's just great. Well, I hope you enjoyed yourself because this will be the last time you'll ever see him."

"What?" Arynne finally managed to say.

Ecstasy sighed. She seemed to do that a lot. Then she took a step closer and gave Arynne a fake smile. "Look sweetie, I don't know who you are, and, honestly, I don't care, but let me just tell you this in the hopes that it prevents you from some future suffering and way too many mistakes. You are not any more important to him than any of the other women he's ever been with. Believe me, I've seen a lot of them come and go, and you know who is still here? Me."

"I'm not... we're not in competition," Arynne said, still not getting a handle on the situation.

With a smug smile, the manager straightened. "That's right. We're not. Good. You're smarter than the average."

"Dion wouldn't do that to me," Arynne said, not processing whatever this witch was saying.

Her smile fell, and she *tsk*ed sharply then moved in, using her physical presence to back Arynne up across the space toward the glass windows. "Oh, you idiot. It isn't like that at all. Dion is a sweet guy. He's sweet like a puppy. He loves everybody, he doesn't want anybody to get hurt, and he does more things than he should for people he doesn't even know. Thinks he can save the world, and then those he helps want too much from him, and I have to swoop in and fix everything because that is what I do. I fix things for him. I make it all better, and that is why he is always going to need me. To clean up mess-ups like you."

Arynne finally bumped against the windows with nowhere left to go. The other woman just kept on coming, physically pressing herself against Arynne.

"Get off me!" Arynne cried, unsure but terrified at what was happening.

"And believe me, honey, you are one mess I wouldn't mind cleaning up," Ecstasy purred, her voice turning husky with clear sexual intent and equal parts menace. She grabbed for Arynne's hips to pull her closer. That's when Ecstasy felt Arynne's belly.

Screeching, the woman leapt away like a startled cat. "Holy crap, are you pregnant?!"

"Yes!" Arynne said, bringing her hands in front of herself as if she were trying to protect her baby from this witch of a woman. Arynne was near tears, but she tried to clamp down on them.

"Is it his?" the manager demanded harshly, her professional persona returning.

"No!" Arynne answered honestly, an irrational fear taking her mind that somehow this woman would take her baby from her.

"Oh, thank gods," Ecstasy declared, noticeably relieved. "Then that's just a different problem. I'll have to have you sign ... I don't know ... something ... that declares Dion not the father." She flipped open her phone again and started typing furiously on it. "And of course, the lawyers will charge me a freaking fortune just to spend twenty minutes answering a simple fucking question."

"What are you doing?" Dion asked, returning with his guitar case in hand. He looked between his manager and Arynne, who were both now ten feet away from where he had left them.

Ecstasy immediately plastered her fake, pixie-girl smile back on. "Nothing. I was admiring the view. This place is amazing," she stated.

"Yeah, it is," he agreed warily, his eyes darting to Arynne. She pushed herself off the glass door and came over to him but didn't take his hand when he offered it.

He was leaving her.

He lowered his hand.

"X, can you wait for me outside?" he asked, softly.

"Sure, no problem," his manager said matching his tone, then when she passed him, she paused. "You want me to take your guitar out to the car?"

"Yeah, sure. Thanks," he said, but his eyes didn't leave Arynne.

It was enough for Ecstasy as she shot one last satisfied glance back at Arynne, then went to get his guitar case and left without a single courteous word of goodbye.

The house felt cavernous now as only the two of them stood saying nothing to each other.

When the screaming silence became unbearable, she turned away.

"Have a nice trip," Arynne said, thinking it would sound nonchalant and grown-up in the bigger person sort of way, but it just sounded hollow.

"Arynne," Dion said, but he stumbled when she moved away.

"How long are you going to be gone?" she asked, trying and failing, to keep her voice level.

The breath fell out of him in a huff. "The tour is for six months. I'll be on the road the entire time."

Arynne could see what the manager meant then. There was no way his attention wouldn't drift away in that sort of time.

At least this is better than when Thomas left, she thought, but it didn't feel better. She had wanted to be done comparing them, and here she was doing it again.

"It'll just be me now," she said softly. Gently, she pressed her hands against her abdomen. *It was always going to be just us,* she thought.

"God, Arynne. I don't want to go. I just..." He spun in place, clearly frustrated. "I have to. I made promises and... and I should have talked with you about it."

Arynne forced a smile. "No, no. You don't owe me anything. I mean a heads up would have been nice, but I get it. You have to go. Thank you, for everything, I guess."

She wanted him to say he would come back, and when he didn't, she forced herself to meet his eyes and ask.

"Will you be coming back?" she asked.

"I... someday," he admitted lamely.

Arynne nodded. "Okay, have a good trip." She turned then and headed upstairs to her room, swallowing her feelings. She thought he would call after her or follow, but she made it all the way to her room, and he did neither. Once the door was at her back, she thought she would cry, or scream, or wail. She could feel those things inside trying to get out.

Nothing came. Only silence.

Sliding down the door, she tried to wrap her arms around her legs, but her belly prevented it.

Somewhere far away, she thought she heard the front door shut. She imagined the car door following a few moments later and it rolling down the private drive, through the security gates and away, never to return.

19

Dion whipped his hair back as the camera pushed in on his face. Whoever had used their phone to film the concert had done a terrible job since most of the images bounced and jostled enough to make Arynne seasick, but she had endured it to get to this moment. Dion looked out across the stadium full of bodies, all churning and cheering with him in their bacchic ecstasy. He had lost his shirt at some point in the performance, and it added to his mystique. To Arynne's eyes though, he looked tired in the way he leaned on his microphone stand, gripping the microphone itself as if it were his last lifeline.

Shifting on her bed, Arynne's enormous belly rolled with the small life inside her, making the laptop she had balanced on top nearly slide off completely.

"That's enough, baby," she said in mock irritation, lifting her laptop off, but then she looked down in amazement as the fabric of her large pajama shirt revealed a perfect little mitten-shaped hand pressing up through her stomach. Passing her own finger over the little palm, she breathed out in giggly awe. At the touch, the little hand darted back, returning her stomach to a smooth roundness.

"Soon, baby," Arynne said and returned to her video. The concert had been three days ago, and Arynne clicked through the playlist she had subscribed to, looking through each video in turn. A whole half year summarized as a series of clips. Dion was in each of them, differentiated only by what he was or wasn't wearing. There were interviews on late night shows and concerts galore that she had seen dozens of times. Thumbing through them all again, she wondered for the hundredth time what she thought she was doing when a notice popped up in the corner of her screen.

It was an alert informing her that someone had used a security code to get past the front gate. While she was pretty sure she knew who it was, she clicked the link for the security camera just the same to check. In a field of gray, a gray car sat at the gate, waiting for it to retract open enough to drive through. Sure enough, Eileen and Zephyr sat in the seat of Zephyr's conservative car. He tapped at the steering wheel with impatient thumbs while Eileen seemed to be talking animatedly, if silently, since it was a picture feed only.

Almost time for her prenatal check. Arynne and baby had just entered the final trimester, and Eileen had been coming every week to check on her. And to tell her how her torrid love affair with a local island shaman who was also a really good Elvis impersonator was going.

Sighing, Arynne set aside her computer and waggled her way up to standing to go greet her guests. By the time she got over to the spiral staircase and had started working her way down it, they opened the front door to drag in suitcases.

"What's going on?" Arynne called.

"We're moving in!" Eileen declared, opening her arms for a hug.

Zephyr saluted before going back out to grab two more bags.

"What do you mean, 'moving in?'" Arynne asked as she made it to the bottom of the stairs.

"That's it! I quit!" Zephyr declared in a loud voice. "I'm just going to burn it down and collect the insurance money. Do you know any good arsonists?"

Arynne waddled up to Eileen, who had been patiently waiting, and leaned in to hug her. "Is he talking about the hotel?"

"Non-stop since he picked me up," Eileen confirmed in her ear.

"I'm pretty sure you can't collect the insurance money if you burn it down yourself," Arynne said.

"Yeah, but if you don't tell them, who's to know?" he countered.

Arynne shrugged one shoulder. "Good point. So..." She took in the pile of luggage. "You two are annexing my home?"

"We talked about it, and since the baby could come soon, we decided that it would be better that you weren't here in this big place alone," Zephyr said, his gruff exterior doing nothing to hide his gooey center.

"We're here to wait on you hand and foot. I am your maid, and he will be your butler," Eileen chimed in.

"My butler?" Arynne laughed.

Zephyr rolled his eyes. "And chef and housekeeper and whatever else needs doing around here." He then looked around the space as if seeing it for the first time. "Oh. It's clean."

"It's more than clean, dear lord Zephyr," Eileen chided, picking up two of her bags. "What did you think she was doing out here all this time?"

"Well, I don't know. I've been trapped under a hotel this last year," Zephyr countered, kicking the last bag, his own, in through the door before slamming it shut. "I'll take my bags up later. I gotta cook something."

He picked up a paper bag from among the luggage and charged to the kitchen with it.

"What are you going to make?" Arynne called after, trying to get the motivation to follow, but the prospect of trying to sit on one of the stools in her current state seemed impossible.

"It's gooey, delicious, and bad for you. Everything comfort food should be," Zephyr said as he proceeded to pull a variety of cheese out of his bag. "Only I do it with special cheeses so it's also fancy."

Eileen took herself over to the dining room table, now polished to a mirror shine, and Arynne decided that was far more reasonable.

"Yeah, but what is it?" Arynne asked.

"Enchilada mac and cheese casserole."

The two women stared at him as he dug out a cheese grater.

"That sounds amazing, actually," Arynne said.

"Told you," Zephyr replied and returned his focus on his preparations.

Eileen and Arynne shared a grin as Zephyr attacked the cooking preparations like he was a general at war.

"Okay, now, first thing," Eileen said. "We do not have to stay with you here in the big house if you don't want us to. I'm perfectly happy to take up one of the many luxury... I don't know, what do you call them? Cabins? I would call them cabins if we were in Minnesota, but on a tropical island, who knows?"

"Guest houses," Arynne said confidently, then shrugged. "That's what we called them in my father's estate, at least."

"That works for me. Sounds very sophisticated. I guess we're all sophisticated now," Eileen agreed.

Arynne shook her head, smiling as she let her gaze drift out the large window over the tropical waterfall pond. Twilight had settled in, painting the skies gorgeous oranges and coral pinks. The lights in the darker, shadowed pool were matching them at the moment, Arynne having long discovered the controls to change up the lighting programmed under the water.

Eileen was silent for a moment in thought, then she asked, "Did Dion ever tell you about our life before his fame and fortune changed everything?"

"No," Arynne said dreamily. "Not much any way. He didn't talk too much about his past before he left. At least, I think we would have needed more than a week to get into it."

"Do you miss him?" Eileen asked, matching her dream-like tone, then she amended, "Nevermind. I can see that you do."

"He calls," Arynne defended. "Every so often when he has time. Just to check in. Maybe to tell me how things are going with him."

Arynne could feel Eileen's next question, so she continued before she could ask it. "I'm not angry with him. He is a good person who helped me out when I needed it, but he doesn't owe me anything. Nobody does. I'm very content with my life here, and I'm very grateful to him."

"Is that little speech one you've practiced or is it how you really feel?" Zephyr piped in, obviously overhearing even though he didn't appear to be.

"Both?" Arynne called, but she didn't want to talk about it, so she changed the subject. "And as far as I'm concerned, you can both stay in the house. There are plenty of rooms here, and you are right. I'm getting closer to show time with this little one."

The midwife beamed at Arynne, making the younger woman shift in place. "What?" she asked, unsure of the attention.

"You are going to be a wonderful mother," Eileen said, leaning over to touch Arynne's knee with a gentle hand. The gesture reminded Arynne of one of her nannies growing up, a kind woman who gave wonderful hugs, but whose name Arynne struggled to remember. She had left them when Arynne turned six, and the sudden memory made her wonder if she could ever find her again.

"This will be ready in twenty minutes," Zephyr interjected again, blowing on a pot of over-bubbling water that he had been neglecting while browning some hamburger. All the smells were making Arynne's mouth water.

Arynne smiled at her only friends in the whole world. Though she knew Dion was never coming back, she was grateful for what he left her.

Eileen patted her hand. "A new life is beginning for you soon, little mother. I'm glad we can be here to help you with it."

She remembered the feel of his hands on her, the touch of his lips. She traced her own breasts through her shirt, recalling the exact pressure he squeezed there, then she slipped his dildo between her folds. Her whole body came alive in the memory. While the sensations were a quarter of what they had been, she hung on to the fragments of fantasy while she worked the shaft in and out of herself. Her breath quickened, and she felt herself climbing. With her free hand, she grabbed a pillow and covered her mouth, so she didn't make any sounds.

She thought of him thrusting inside her, just touching the ache inside herself. She could faintly hear the sound of his moans as he did it faster and faster. She wanted him to come back to her; she would forgive him if he did.

"Dion," she whispered, pushing away the feelings of inadequacy that came when she did this, trying to focus on the sexier thoughts. Why wasn't she good enough? Why didn't the men in her life want her in return? Was it her fault in some way? If she had only told him how she had felt about him... but she hadn't really known at the time. It had been too soon, and her feelings were too muddled. Would it have made a difference?

The memory continued to fray, like rotten strands disintegrating in her hands even as she struggled to hold them together.

"No, no, no," she hissed, but it was no use. Everything she did was failing her. Discouraged, she removed the useless toy and threw it across the room.

The house did not stir.

Not too far away, in their own bedrooms, Zephyr and Eileen had gone to sleep hours ago. Or she assumed they had. Zephyr had declared himself tired and fed up with life, which he had repeated ad nauseam for the past week. Eileen always went to bed early. So here Arynne was with her tattered memories and head full of useless, pointless regrets.

Curling on her side with a pillow stuffed under her belly for support, Arynne stared out at the large moon reflecting on the ocean below. She wondered if she was going to need to leave the estate she had made her home, if everything in it would remind her of him.

"I don't want to be a bitter old woman," she said softly to the moon. The moon did not respond, only hung serenely in the star-filled sky, shining mysteriously down on the world and its secrets.

It was only then, as Arynne's breathing slowed, and she started to drift to sleep, that she realized she heard something on the edge of the silence.

Somewhere ... someone was playing music?

Arynne crept along the balcony that lined the interior's second floor, her heart pounding out of her chest. Below, she heard bangs, crashes, and laughter. It never occurred to her that they could be robbed, but the singular truth that although there were three people in the house, none of them were very equipped to handle more than a crazed squirrel attack, and it hit home how vulnerable she really was. She hadn't even locked the front door since there was a bricked fence with spikes on the top blocking off their tiny finger of the island. And based on the shadows dancing below, a least a dozen people were piling in through her door.

So how did these hooligans get in? Maybe they weren't really robbers, but teenagers crashing a house they thought was abandoned? They sounded like high schoolers.

Taking a shaking breath, she debated her options. She had her phone clutched in her hand, so she could call the police. She glanced up at the other doors where she knew Eileen and Zephyr were sleeping. Didn't they hear any of this? She didn't dare call out to them.

Running back to the master suite and locking the door until help arrived was a choice.

Before she could get up the nerve to do either of those things, the place echoed with more laughter. There were *more* people filing in! The place echoed louder. Someone was strumming a guitar?

Carefully, Arynne waddled over to the edge of the balcony and carefully looked over the side in a slow, measured way that hopefully wouldn't attract attention by the crowd below.

The first thing to come into sight was a pile of ... luggage? In the middle of the pile, a pair of humans were writhing and making out. Several more people were filing in through the open front door. Another pair of women laughed and pointed at the two lovebirds in the luggage pile, and a third woman stood nearby talking business-like on the phone.

That woman Arynne recognized.

"Ecstasy?"

Arynne's heart sped up to a rapid tattoo as she realized what that woman's presence meant.

"Dion," she breathed and turned to rush down the spiral steps. Or she would have if she could have done anything more than wobble. She encountered two women trying to come up the spiral stairs, whose laughter was cut short when the caught sight of her.

"Who the hell are you?" one asked, her hair so teased and sprayed that she looked like she had stuck her finger in a light socket.

"Dear lord, you look ready to pop," the other woman said, staring at Arynne's belly.

"Where's Dion?" Arynne asked, ignoring them.

"Down there," the first woman gestured, then got out of the way as Arynne pushed past them.

"Hey, wait for me!" a third woman called at the bottom, only to jump out of her skin "Holy Hell!"

Feeling like an awkward tugboat, Arynne kept moving, wading through the strangers, most of them women, milling, drinking, and smoking in her house!

Through the front door, three burly men filed in carrying equipment and bags, weaving through the half dozen other people laughing as they shared a wine bottle between the door and the pile. The whole room started hooting and cheering the couple among the bags, inspiring two others to start their own makeout fest on the dining room table.

Then one of the party started peeing into one of the cups of the fountain. "Gods, Rhonda, use a bathroom!" one of the partiers shouted.

"Where the hell is one in this place?" the pee-er argued.

"What the hell?!" Arynne shouted this time. Her voice rang off the walls as she marched straight up to the offending woman to yank her off the edge of the cup of the fountain, the smell of pee thick in the air. "What the hell do you think you are doing?!"

"Whoa, get off me, bitch!" the woman shouted.

Half the group went quiet, the ones who seemed sober anyway, and all stared at her as a united wall of eyes. Arynne almost flinched, but anger fueled her, and she spun around to meet every eye as if daring them.

"What is wrong with all of you?" she said to the nearest group milling about by her. "What are you doing here? Where's Dion?"

"Who the hell are you?" one of them asked.

"I live here!" Arynne said, then tripped on a bag that someone dropped at her feet. Her arms cartwheeled for a second but failed to help her recover her balance, and she flopped into the pile of bags like a beached whale.

Everyone staring at her laughed at the sight of her feet going up in the air as she landed back on an actually very soft duffel bag. Any panic she had about hurting herself blew away as she continued to sink in among the bags themselves like bulky quicksand.

"Oh Dion!" the woman in the couple next to her cried out as she grabbed at the man's face to continue their passionate kiss. Then they both stopped and turned their heads to look at Arynne, now lying inches away from them.

"Who the hell are you?" the woman asked.

Arynne laid there, unable to form a sentence, she was so stunned. Her eyes locked with Dion's which went through a spectrum of happiness, alarm, and confusion.

"Arynne, are you alright?" he asked.

"Yes," she said with a small voice, even though she had no reason to think it was true.

Before they could say any more, the woman on top of Dion grabbed his face to turn it her way.

"Hey, pay attention to me. It's my turn now," she said with an obnoxious pout.

Ecstasy moved to stand in front of Arynne, practically standing over her. The manager clapped her hands twice, taking instant command of the room. "Alright, alright, that's enough. I don't got time for this shit. I'm exhausted. Okay, I need everyone to just find themselves a bedroom and claim it, except for the master bedroom and whatever one is right next to it because that shit is mine. I don't care where you end up. Sort it out yourselves."

The crowd turned to obey, and Ecstasy grinned maliciously down on Arynne, who had failed to invoke a tenth of the same reaction.

"What are you doing lying on the bags?" she asked in that stupid sweet voice of hers.

"I..." Arynne started, but she really didn't know what to say. She tried to sit up, but since her stomach muscles were long gone, she found it nearly impossible. Ecstasy watched her with a critical eye as she struggled and then threw up her hands. "Oh, for God's sake, Brutus, help the weebo woman stand up." And she turned to walk away, kicking at the foot in her path with her own high-heeled shoe. "Dion, get up!"

The woman on top of Dion cackled in response.

"Corrina, seriously, get off me!" Dion barked, bordering on shouted, even as he laughed.

One of the burly men finally came over and grabbed the woman still pinning the rock god down, dragging her off of him. Laughing, Dion sat up, looked directly at Arynne, continuing to grin drunkenly.

Arynne's heart leapt into her throat. He had been gone for months, so it wasn't like he was going to change all that much in that time, and yet, she wasn't sure she recognized him. While she had seen his face in those videos, it wasn't the same as seeing him staring up at her, reeking of alcohol and exhaustion. His eyes were rimmed red, and he looked greasy, with a general unwell pallor.

Arynne thought she would throw up from the overwhelming smell of it all.

"Look at her. She's starstruck," one of the crowd jeered, and they all laughed.

Another of the burly men stepped up and offered the superstar a hand to pull him to his feet.

Then Dion turned and offered his hand to Arynne and waited. Arynne stared at it. This was not the reunion she had ever imagined, not in a million years.

The room had continued to stare and watch, though several had claimed bags and made their way up to the balcony. Those watched from above, like gallery patrons at ye olde theater, anticipation all over their faces as they watched what fresh drama was about to happen.

"Dion! What the hell?" Eileen called from above, interrupting their little tableau. All of the intruder's eyes shifted up to the older woman wearing a nightgown and flowery robe, her silver hair down as she leaned over the balcony. "Why do I have strangers invading my room?"

"Oh, sorry, Eileen. I forgot you were going to be here," Dion said, crouching down to take Arynne's hand and elbow, all while keeping his attention on his cousin.

Eileen turned just as the two women who had woken her up tried to move past her into the room to claim it. "I don't think so, sweethearts," she snapped, blocking their way in.

"Find another room, Starfire and Coriander," Ecstasy snapped, already back on her cellphone.

"But all the rooms are taken," one of the women whined.

"Then go claim a guest cottage outside. There are dozens of them, dammit. Do I have to do all your thinking for you?" Ecstasy snapped before spinning in place as whoever she was calling answered, flipping instantly into her sicky sweet voice. "Yes, hi, this is Ecstasy representing Dionysus. With whom am I speaking?"

All while this was happening, Arynne had leveraged herself back to her feet with Dion's help, though she retracted her hand from his as soon as she was steady. He didn't seem to notice; his focus was instead on her large belly.

"Are you okay?" he asked, reaching out to put a hand on her stomach without asking.

"Yes, I'm fine," she said tersely, backing away from his hand.

She folded her arms across her chest. "Why didn't you call to say you were coming?" she asked.

I would have had time to prepare my heart for seeing you again, she thought.

He blinked as if waking up from a dream and hadn't seemed to notice her retreat. "Yeah, well, I don't really plan too much ahead of time. Just not in my nature." The room returned his grin with added jovial nods and chuckles. "That's what I got her for. Ecstasy, is everything sorted?"

The manager barely turned to wave a hand while nodding, still talking a mile a minute.

"I have at least twenty-three people here who are going to need bedrooms. Can we accommodate them all?" Dion asked.

"Uh, yes, I think so," Arynne said. "But who are all these people?"

"My Bacchanalia," Dion said as if that explained anything. "My entourage."

"His harem!" one of the women called as she came back to retrieve a bag from the pile.

"No, absolutely not," Dion said, laughing, then looked to Arynne, the first hint of worry quirking his eyebrows. "Don't worry about all of them. This is just part of the image, you know. The marketing. It doesn't mean..." But he trailed off, as if he had never thought about what it meant before.

Ecstasy reappeared next to the pile, kicking two bags and a familiar guitar case away from the pile. "Brutus. This one is Dion's. Take it up to the master bedroom," she ordered. "Then come back down and get mine. I have to make a dozen more fucking calls."

A look of guilt crossed Dion's face. "Thank you, X," he tried to say, but she stopped and pointed a finger in his face.

"Just don't talk to me for forty-eight hours. If there is going to be one good freaking thing to come out of canceling Paris ... Paris! then it's going to be *me* getting to sleep without having to talk to Your. Stupid. Face."

"Hey, I found the master suite! Come check it out. It's sick!" A voice, the woman Dion had called Corrina, shouted from above.

And to Arynne's horror, that was when she remembered that she had left Dion's dildo out on the floor.

21

"Get out!" Arynne shouted before she even got into her—the master bedroom. "Get the hell out!"

"Excuse me?" Corrina challenged, setting her fists on her hips.

"Get out," Arynne repeated, grinding her teeth as she pointed for the door.

The other woman scoffed and turned to the door. "Dion," she whined. "This bitch is trying to kick me out of our room!"

Fantasies of seizing the woman by her overly teased hair and ripping it out flashed through Arynne's mind.

"Corrina..." Dion started, but Ecstasy charged in.

"Dion needs to sleep, so you're going to have to find somewhere else to park your ass tonight," the woman said in no uncertain terms.

"But Dion—" Corrine tried again, but Ecstasy snapped her phone open as sharply as a slap.

"Or I can get you a flight home tonight," she said.

The woman looked to Dion with pleading puppy-dog eyes, but he didn't look at her as he moved toward the bathroom.

"I gotta piss," he said dully and disappeared, leaving the three women behind to sort it out. Arynne couldn't believe that he was passively dodging the issue like that. Ecstasy didn't seem at all surprised and lifted her chin proudly as she looked down her nose at the helpless Corinna.

With no other options, Corinna blew out a dramatic sigh and grabbed her bag. "Fine," she snapped childishly, then turned on her heel and marched out of the room.

"You, too, fatty," Ecstasy said to Arynne. "He needs to sleep."

"This is my room," Arynne said softly, but she knew it wasn't. It was so clear that she had gotten too comfortable, too trusting, relying on Dion's generosity. She felt so exhausted, drooping on her feet. Her head pounded, and she just wanted to lie down.

"She's fine," Dion called from the bathroom, chorused by the sound of liquid hitting water. "Just go find your own bed, X. You're done for the night."

Ecstasy scoffed at that. "You wish." She shot a glare at Arynne but turned to go out the bedroom door. "Fine. He can deal with you."

The manager passed Eileen with Zephyr trailing behind as they came in.

"Where's Dion?" Eileen demanded, folding her arms across her chest like a parent who had her last straw trampled on.

Arynne jutted a thumb toward the bathroom, not daring to look his way.

Eileen had no such reservations. She marched straight over to the bathroom door, her arms stringently folded. "What the hell do you think you are doing?"

"Trying to not think about you standing there," Dion responded, shortly followed by a flush. The sound of the running water made Arynne's own bladder activate with urgent need. The baby within her started wiggling on it, making the need more urgent.

Just hold on, she thought at her baby. *Mommy needs to wait.'*

"Look, I'm sorry about the chaos..." Dion's voice drifted from the bathroom.

"Jesus, Dion. You look like hell!" Eileen exclaimed, her folded arms dropping as Arynne presumed Dion turned around.

"I feel like hell," Dion admitted.

Arynne glanced at Zephyr, who rubbed his temples like he had a headache.

"Look, I know how this all looks, but this was the only way I could get home. You don't know... you don't understand all the pressures I'm under right now," Dion continued in a softer voice. Arynne moved to sit on the bed but forgot that the sink faced the open space between the bedroom and the bathroom. Dion stood there, staring out the window as he washed his hands, only to perk up when she came into view.

Dammit, she should have just stayed where she was. As much as she had missed him, she felt surprised that she didn't want to see him. The images of the women, his bacchanalia, that he had come with, their contempt and judgement, rained down on her. She could sense the pecking order mentality amongst them all in relation to this one man, to Dion. It disgusted her. She was just another woman among them all to him; she could see that clearly now. Her secret hopes that they could ever be something more, the story she told herself that he just needed to get this tour done, and then when he came back, they would talk, disintegrated, all in the moment that he looked at her. Or maybe it had happened when she had first locked eyes with him in the luggage pile with Corinna straddling him, basically fucking him for all to see.

She couldn't return the grin he was giving her but shifted instead to go stand next to Zephyr. "I don't know what to do," she said softly to the man who leaned in to hear her. "Should I just grab all my stuff and sleep elsewhere tonight?"

"No, absolutely not," Zephyr said, harshly, clearly angry. "*You* are staying here. I'll kick his ass out onto the terrace if I have to. I don't know of any kind of asshole that would throw a pregnant woman out of her bed in the middle of the goddam night." His quietly seething rage helped Arynne feel better, like it justified her own. Eileen and Dion exchanged a few more words, but they were too quiet, and the running water drowned them out.

It was fine. She kept telling herself she didn't care. She just needed to endure things until he was done and out of her room.

At last, Dion and Eileen exited the bathroom. Eileen for her part headed for the door. "Okay, well, there is nothing for it but to go back to sleep, so I will finish chewing you out in the morning."

"Hey, Zeph! Glad to see you. How's the hotel working out?" Dion asked, moving to grasp Zephyr's hand, but the other man avoided it. He turned to Arynne. "Do you want me to throw him out?" he asked her.

"No, no," Arynne replied. "I need... I need to talk to him first. You can go to bed, really."

"Alright," Zephyr relented, still seething. "If you change your mind, just call."

She nodded and her last ally left, presumably to go to bed.

Arynne continued to stand there, her arms wrapped around herself while she stared at the floor. The toes of his boots came into view, and she could feel his presence like a feverish heat wave in front of her.

"Arynne," he said softly.

She hadn't wanted to look up, but her eyes lifted on their own accord anyway.

She could see him holding himself back, his eyes pleading. But pleading for what?

"What do you want from me?" she asked, her voice coming out dark and angry.

"I'm so sorry," he whispered.

Her chin jutted out. "Do you even know what you're sorry for?"

He lifted his hands to press the heels into his eyes. "So many damn things," he said wearily. He stepped back from her several paces until the backs of his thighs hit the edge of the bed. The platform made it awkward, and he half fell back toward the floor only to do a stumble skip to save himself.

"You're not sleeping here," Arynne told him, alarmed at his motion. They weren't together, even if they had slept together for a week, so it was pretty presumptuous of him to assume it.

"No, I know," he assured her, dropping his elbows to rest them on his knees so he could lean forward. "I need to talk to you first, and then I'll go out to the gazebo or something."

Maybe it was mention of the gazebo and its special significance to her, but Arynne felt some of her anger drain out.

"What do you need to talk about, and is it going to take long? I need to go to the bathroom, and you look like you'll be asleep before I get back," she stated. It was true. Her baby had been dancing on her bladder ever since she had fallen on her butt, and the need was still inconveniently urgent.

"I won't fall asleep. I promise," he said, waving toward the bathroom. "Go ahead. I'll be awake when you come back."

"If you're sure," she said, already moving in that direction.

His nod was more like an up and down shaking of a pom-pom as he let it hang nearly to his knees, and Arynne had to resist the urge to go to him to set a hand on that weary head. What she wanted to do was wrap herself in his arms and breathe him in. She had missed him so much, and she was worried about him. He was unwell. She could see it, and she cared.

She cared.

"I'll be right back," she said, tearing herself away from temptation.

"I'm sorry I didn't call more often," Dion called. "I did mean to..." Arynne could hear that he was still talking, but his words disintegrated under the sounds of her using the bathroom.

"I can't hear you," she called. "Just wait."

"I'm not asleep," he called back.

Sighing, Arynne got up and went to the sink to wash her hands.

She half expected to find him curled up and asleep on her bed, but he continued to sit there, his head wavering as he fought against the pull.

"Dion, you're in no shape to talk now," she chided, but he didn't respond. "Dion? Dion!"

He jerked up, snorting crudely. "No, I..." was all he got out before his speech deteriorated back into useless garbles.

Arynne shook her head and crossed to him to take his hands. He waved at her as she approached. "It's okay. Lay down," she said, soothingly.

"I got to talk..."

"I'll still be here in the morning," she assured. "We can talk then. Just lie down."

He yielded then, letting her guide him to his side on the bed with a flop. She seized his boots and yanked them off so he would be more comfortable. She pulled her blanket up over him. Then gazed down on his face. Now that he was unconscious, she dared to slide her hand over his hair. It felt greasy and overly full of product, clearly in need of a shower. Yet, all she felt was concern for him. How hard was it living on the road like he had that he should come back so broken like this?

Now that he was down, the weight of her own exhaustion settled on her overburdened form.

"Screw it," she said softly and went around the bed to lever herself onto the other side. She didn't want to think about what this meant. Lying down, she positioned her belly support pillow between them and tucked her arm under her head pillow. He slept through the whole jostling, his face in a soft repose. His sleeping face reminded her of a sleeping boy, innocent and trusting, complete with his hand curled up by his nose.

Her heart ached.

Why did this all have to be so complicated? Arynne thought. It was one thing to miss him, to dream about him. But this reality lying next to her that had flooded the house she had painstakingly, and in recent weeks, slowly, restored to something not just livable, but beautiful... was this what she wanted to deal with?

Slowly, she laced her fingers in between his loose ones. "I want to go back to before you left," she whispered. "I want you to have stayed and for us to fall in love and for me to be the only woman..."

She stopped at that thought. *The only woman in his life?*

No.

She wanted Eileen around, and she could imagine a dozen other scenarios where other women would be a part of his life.

Outside her door, piercing laughter penetrated the door.

Arynne pulled her hand away and tucked it back under her pillow. Dion didn't stir at all. She closed her eyes and waited for sleep.

They could deal with things in the morning.

22

When Arynne came back to consciousness, it was to the sound of broken glass. She had no real memory of falling asleep; she felt like she had lain awake for a long time, listening to every antic and imagining every bit of destruction the bacchanalia wrought on everything she had spent so much time and energy restoring.

Just when she had begun to feel safe, she was reminded that just like in her father's house, this too did not truly belong to her.

It belonged to the man lying next to her.

She almost laid her head back down to try to find a few more minutes of sleep, but remembering Dion's actual presence sped her up to wakefulness. She had turned over in the night to face away from the center, and she had to twist or try to twist. The baby within her pushed and wiggled in protest, but Arynne managed to look over her shoulder at the other side of the bed.

He was still there.

His back was to her as he lay curled up on his side. At some point, her unwelcome visitor had managed to pull off the leather jacket he had been wearing to reveal the black tank he had on underneath. His bare shoulder with its one mole peeking out from the material looked so intimate for some reason.

She imagined herself moving up to put her front to his back and slipping her fingers into that space made by the cloth before stroking down that warm skin in a loving caress. In that position, she could place her nose at the nape of his neck and breathe in the scent of his hair. Just setting her cheek against his back and closing her eyes to capture those few moments more of sleep re-enflamed the ache in her heart.

Gods, she had missed him. She almost convinced herself to do it because then maybe he would wake up and give her answers or at least explain his statement last night—that there was something he needed to tell her. But the baby continued to wiggle hard within her, and her bladder had reached screaming urgency.

"I hate being pregnant," she said, muttering the truism under her breath as she rolled up and out.

Once she had tended her needs in the bathroom, a cackle of laughter rang out through the door, completely heedless of anyone who could still be sleeping. Needing to know what was going on and discovering if there was anything she could do about it, Arynne belted on a bathrobe. The terrycloth did not cover her belly anymore, but it did obscure it, and that would have to be good enough for now.

Quietly, she shut the door behind her and went to the balcony to get an initial survey of down below.

The main room appeared to still be empty, but the hum of talking echoed up the space along with a discordant undercurrent of someone cooking in the kitchen.

Chapter 22

Arynne had braced herself for whatever manner of mess she might encounter when she made it downstairs. And yet, she was still shocked when she walked into the kitchen area.

It was like a bomb had gone off.

The formally immaculate space had splatters of food everywhere, wet, dry and otherwise. Bottles of alcohol she had never brought into the house were clustered on every counter. Across the floor was the source of the crash that had awoken her originally, the glass bottle of milk she had bought from the store smashed all over the floor with a splat of white large enough to lie down in.

Four people occupied the space. One of them was a woman wearing a skin-tight leotard with make-up smeared around her eyes sitting at the counter. She had obviously gone to sleep with it on. A second woman stood near her, dressed in baggy black with chains coming not just off her pants, but hanging from her ear to nose as well. Despite her darker look, she talked animatedly as she dumped more pancake mix into a large bowl that already had a slurry of the stuff which she stirred with the other hand. One of the burly men ignored everything to read a newspaper. The fourth person had taken up residence against the back counter, pouring what appeared to be bourbon into her coffee. Her hair hung in face like a near curtain as if to hide her from the light.

And they all just ignored the mess all around them, including the milk still crawling across the floor.

"What the hell are you doing!?" Arynne cried. All four occupants stopped and turned to stare at her. Somehow, it only made her madder.

The one cooking broke the silence a moment later. "Oh, hey, there's spilt milk over here," she reported as if this was normal.

That was it.

That was all she said before she went back to the conversation she was having with the leotard woman at the counter.

"So anyway, I said to her—"

"I see that!" Arynne continued angrily, her sharpness interrupting their conversation again. They both looked at her, offended by the interruption.

"Yeah, well, maybe you should do something about that," the one cooking said snidely and clicked on one of the burners of the oven to set a flat griddle pan on it.

"Excuse me?" Arynne retorted, making it very clear that she had no intention of doing that, even if she could get her bulky self all the way down to the floor. She couldn't even tie her shoes anymore!

They eyed her again. "Oh, for gods' sake," the one sitting at the counter said while the burly one with a newspaper peeked at her over the edge of the paper before flicking it back to straight to continue reading.

"Someone is looking to get fired," the one that had been pouring bourbon in her coffee noted with dry sarcasm.

"Yeah, no kidding," the woman at the counter agreed.

"Look, housekeeper," the cook said, pointing the whisk at her like a baton, which flung around bits of batter to add to the mess. "You're lucky I am covering your ass by making breakfast. The least you can freaking do is be grateful and do your damn job."

Arynne's blood boiled. "I am not a housekeeper!"

She marched to the fridge and yanked it open. It looked like another smaller bomb had gone off inside. Her carefully organized food containers had been half opened, partly dumped, or put back empty.

The two women exchanged glances with each other. "Then who are you?" the one at the counter asked.

"She thinks she's the one that Dion is going to choose above all others, fall in love with, and live happily ever after," Ecstasy said as she stepped past Arynne. The manager gave her a smug smile as she stretched her arms overhead. "Good morning, bitches. Charlie, what the heck are you making?"

She leaned past the one cooking to look into the bowl as she grabbed the woman by the hips and pulled her back intimately, almost upsetting the bowl.

"Pancakes," Charlie said breathlessly, then tipped her head back and was rewarded with a sensual kiss.

"Oh, gross, guys. Not over the food," the bourbon coffee drinker chided before taking a healthy gulp to cover her disgust.

"She wants to do what?" the woman at the counter asked, ignoring what was happening in front of her.

"She's the one who's going to tame the wild Dion. Just ask her," Ecstasy said, breaking the kiss and abandoning her toy for the fridge. "Damn, you guys are pigs. Rhonda, is there coffee?"

"Uh, yes. Trix, where did you get the coffee?" the one at the counter, Rhonda, asked.

Trix moved her backside to reveal the coffee maker. Ecstasy moved in and grabbed the carafe to pour herself a cup. "She even expects him to be step-daddy to her little bastard there."

"Oh, sweetie," Rhonda said, her eyes thick with pity while the one called Charlie started laughing. "You can't fall in love with guys like Dion. They don't belong to anyone."

"He's the freaking son of Zeus, the most notorious womanizer since Tom Jones or Elvis even!" Charlie added.

"I tried to warn her before," Ecstasy said, pulling out a bottle of Arynne's juice to open the top and take a swig straight from the bottle. "But she thinks she's 'the one.'"

"Are you ... pregnant with Dion's child?" Trix asked. Even the bodyguard with the paper lowered it to stare at her.

"No, she's not. I just said she wasn't," Ecstasy said with absolute delight. "Isn't that even more pathetic?"

"Dion?" Rhonda said, raising an eyebrow. "Dion Brewer. A dad. Ha, I can't imagine it."

"You know what your little crush did on the tour?" Ecstasy continued, coming back to the counter with her juice and coffee to lean on it like a cat. "You want to hear about all the little exploits, the leagues of fans throwing their bodies at him left and right, hoping they'll be 'the one' chosen by him? Even if he wanted to pick a 'one and only,' what man in his fucking right mind would be able to resist a buffet like that?"

"Gods, X, you don't have to be crude," Charlie chided and continued to stir before flicking some batter from the end of her spoon on to the griddle. It sizzled and popped.

"Apparently I do because she is just not getting the message. You should just be grateful you got to fuck him at all and move on."

"Oh? She did sleep with him?" Trix asked.

Rhonda sighed. "That does make it harder."

Ecstasy perked up. "Hey, girls, quick show of hands, how many of you have slept with Dion?"

All four of them raised their hands. So did the bodyguard. After a moment, they all broke out laughing.

"My god, look at her face!" Charlie cackled. "Poor little sweet innocent."

This was more than Arynne could take. She knew she was running away, but she didn't care.

"Arynne, wait," Ecstasy called, stopping her just as she made it to the stairs.

Bracing herself, Arynne turned. "What?"

The manager shifted back a half step and slipped her hand into the front pocket of her leather pants. "I just wanted to say ... I'm sorry."

Arynne furrowed her eyebrows harder. "I don't believe you."

Ecstasy laughed. "I don't blame you." Then her eyes drifted down to Arynne's round stomach. "But I do recognize that this situation isn't your fault, really. I mean, what were you supposed to do, with your child on the way and everything? No job, no education—"

"I have an education," Arynne snapped.

"You know what I mean. It's not like you had a lot of options, and if a guy... a man like Dion swept in and offered to save me like that, I'd be an idiot not to take it. I really should have recognized that sooner but..." She sighed and shook her head. "Look. I got issues. And they don't always help me be the best person I can be. So, for everything that I've said to you up until now, I am sorry."

Arynne was taken aback since all of that was true, but it was also the last thing she thought she would hear. "I... thank you," she conceded, though she didn't believe it.

Ecstasy nodded, giving her a small smile. "Look, I just want you to know, I was contacted by a detective a couple of weeks ago." She pulled a card out of her pocket. "I didn't tell him anything about you, but I remembered him last night, and I thought I would just let you know. It's really your choice whether you contact him or not."

Taking the card, Arynne stared down at the simple name embossed in black. Hermes Detective Agency: *We seek what you lost.* An island number was listed underneath. She flipped it over to the back, but there was nothing more written. Someone had tracked her all the way to Dion's band.

"I don't know him," she said, keeping her voice and hands steady. "What would he want?"

Crossing her arms, Ecstasy cocked a thin, perfect eyebrow at her. "Really? You can't think of anyone in the world who would want to find you?"

Gulping back her emotions, Arynne looked down at the card again. "My father," she said softly.

The manager nodded. "Look, I'm just saying, you don't have to have no choices. Your dad is paying for a detective to find you. Probably several but this is the only one that found me. You don't have to stay here; you could go home." Then she raised her hands and took a step back. "But it is completely up to you. You do what's best for you and your baby."

Folding the card into her hand, Arynne could only nod. "Thank you," she said lamely.

Ecstasy returned the nod and took another step back. "I'm going to go back to breakfast now," she said, freeing Arynne from any more obligation to talk to her. Just then several more of Dionysus's entourage came down, laughing and talking. They greeted Ecstasy with cheerful chirps, like morning birds.

Ignoring them all, Arynne continued up the stairs one laborious step at a time. She needed a shower and to get dressed so she could face the challenges all around her. Hoping Dion was still sleeping, Arynne figured she could sneak in and do all those things if she were quick and quiet. But when she pulled the door to the master bedroom opened, she came to a full-stop.

Straddling the rockstar on the bed was the other woman he had been making out with last night. She wore a single t-shirt as a nightgown that someone at some point had cut the neck out of, so that it slipped down her bare shoulders as she seemed to be riding him beneath her. Her back arched as she moaned out loud before both of them turned to look at her.

"Hey!" the woman cried. "Get the fuck out!"

23

Dion didn't really sleep.
Ever.

Except when he had been here on the island.

But since leaving, he couldn't remember even dreaming.

The party just never ended.

Ever.

He had hoped coming back to the island would change that.

He figured he must have slept some, but all he remembered was closing his eyes and then snapping them open the second Corinna dropped down onto his hips.

"Good morning in paradise," she whispered in a sultry voice, leaning forward so the shirt she wore bowed open to flash her tiny but pert breasts at him.

He didn't want this. He just wanted to sleep alone. She was being persistent, and it had been hard enough to tell her "no" once. It just wasn't his nature or his code to tell anyone "no." So much of the good things in his life had come about because he rarely ever said "no."

But this time?

"Corinna," was all he got out and then she stuck her tongue in his mouth, preventing any further requests to get off him.

He didn't kiss her back, but he didn't exactly shove her off either. It was hot, passionate, and mercifully quick. Her smile glowed sensually when she broke the kiss. "I thought this would be a wonderful way to wake up," she purred.

"What time is it?" he asked instead of commenting on that.

"Oh, who cares? Didn't you hear me? We're in paradise! Time has no meaning here," she said, leaning back with a sensual arch, running her hands through her bedroom hair. Her arching exerted pressure on his junk in a rhythm, and he grunted with it involuntarily. It was hard to argue with how it felt since his body had already responded before he had, his sizable erection encouraging her to continue. The view she was giving him was delightful too. He could appreciate the curves and planes of her. He was fairly certain Corinna was older than him, but it didn't matter a single bit. In fact, it just presented an opportunity to learn something new and that rolling circle thing she was doing with her hips was very interesting.

Any other time, he would have just let things play out however they were going to. She was offering this to him, he didn't ask for it, and he was not one to ever say no to a gift. But at that moment, his actual head pounded inside his skull, and the rocking wasn't helping. He was trying to remember something, and as much as his body was enjoying this, his heart and spirit just wasn't in any of it.

Hadn't been in a long time.

Then the woman on him slid backward and crushed his balls.

"Ah! Corinna!" he ground out, grabbing for her hips intending to gently but firmly shove her off. She snagged his hands to lace her fingers between his. He could feel her dampness through his jeans, the musk of her filling his nostrils.

Traitor body, he thought, his erection getting stiffer as she released his hands to flick open the button of his jeans and slide down the zipper. Since he wasn't wearing underwear himself, the head of his dick peeked through the dangerous teeth between them.

A gentle laugh tickled his memory, asking about the dangers of wearing pants without underwear.

Arynne.

Looking around the room, he finally recognized where he was. He wasn't still on the road in some hotel whose name he would never remember. He had come home to the island, to the place he had last felt home and safe. But at that moment he didn't feel it. This wasn't home. This was just another room with another woman he didn't care a bit about.

He wanted Arynne.

"Corinna, please," he meant to beg, but it came out as a growl and sounded more like he was begging for more. It only encouraged her more. He just didn't know *how* to say no. But he needed her to get off.

"Yes," she breathed, as her bud and vulva lips wrapped around his head, riding him without taking him in. "Yes, yes, yes—"

Then the door opened. Both soon to-be-lovers stopped cold, startled by the interruption.

Arynne stood there, her large, dark eyes growing larger.

Dion pushed himself up onto his elbows to see her better. She was here. She was really, truly here.

"Hey!" Corinna cried. "Get the fuck out!"

Arynne startled, her large eyes snapping from him to Corinna, then back to him.

"Arynne, wait—" he started to say, but she didn't. She slammed the door and disappeared.

"What the hell was she thinking, just walking into your room like that?" Corinna said disgustedly.

"Corrina, get off me!" Dion said forcefully this time, finally pushing her off him. As he stood, his pants almost slipped all the way off his hips, and he grabbed at the flaps of denim to struggle the zipper back up. *Dammit, dammit, dammit. This wasn't what I wanted. Fuck. I am an idiot.*

He almost escaped, but Corinna seized his hand. "Wait, where are you going?" she pouted. She glanced at the closed door as if desperately trying to understand. "Are you ... with her...?"

"No, I..." Dion said truthfully. He had no idea what they were, but he only knew that whatever they could be wouldn't be possible if he didn't follow her right now.

"Hey! Whatever it is, it can wait, can't it?" she said as he tried to slip from her hands. Desperately, Corrina grabbed his arm, hooking the elbow and dropping her weight to drag him to a stop.

As he looked down, despite her ridiculous struggling, she shot him another fake, sultry smile. "This is *your* vacation. Let Mama make it a good one for you."

Nothing about her was sultry. Nothing about her was sexy. She was just ridiculous and desperate, and he had never been more repulsed by a woman in his life.

"Get your shit and get out," he growled, finally tearing his hand away.

A memory flashed behind his eyes. Another growl, another angry voice, and his mother in tears as his father physically threw her out of the door of the high-end apartment. She had banged hard against the wall. His father continued to shout about himself, how much he was suffering from their presence.

Dion had been so excited to finally meet his father.

Another memory flashed on its heels: his father coming up behind him on the red carpet, throwing an arm over his shoulders, then boasting to the cameras how much his long-lost son was just like him.

Dion managed to break free from Corinna as she started to cry on the floor.

"No, Dion, please. I'm sorry. I just wanted to make you happy. Please," she begged.

"Oh, gods," he said stumbling back from the visions in his eyes. "I'm my father."

"What is going on here?" Ecstasy demanded, slamming the door open and staring down at the scene before her. How did she always know when he needed her?

He gestured at crying woman on the floor.

"Corrina is leaving," he said tersely. "Get her a first-class ticket to wherever she wants to go."

It was all he got out before he rushed to the bathroom. He barely got to the toilet before the burst of bile exploded from him. He dry-heaved a few moments more, gripping the edge of the high-end porcelain for dear life. Finally, when his guts screamed and his head continued to pound, he lifted his head up and out, resting his cheek on the warm seat looking toward the door.

Eileen stood next to him, leaning against the sink. When she noticed him seeing her, she held out a glass of water to him. Small bubbles danced inside it, leaping off the sides and flying up to burst free of the surface.

"Eileen, I've really fucked up," he said.

"You can't keep going on like this. That's for sure," she said. She shook the glass at him with a waggle.

His arm felt so heavy as he lifted it up to take the water, even though the thought of drinking it at all sounded disgusting. That was just how sick he was.

"Where is she?" he asked.

"Ecstasy took your little friend to get her to pack her things. Two of your muscle men are with her. She's not being very compliant."

"Arynne," he said, but it came out a garble as his tongue stuck to the top of his mouth. He forced a sip to clear it. "I mean Arynne. Where is she?"

Eileen continued to stare at him, her lips pursed together as if they were holding back the words. She crossed her arms against him.

He forced himself to lift his head. "Eileen. Where is she?" he demanded.

Arynne sat looking out over the look out, their look out, next to storage shed. A new fence had been built weeks ago, the fresh, raw wood scent filling her nose as she focused on breathing. Not far away, she could hear the other bacchanalia moving and laughing as they explored the estate gardens and houses. She prayed none of them would find her up there.

The second she had that thought, a rustling came from the nearby foliage, just down the path.

"Dammit," she muttered under her breath as she turned to prepare for the invasion ... of a black cat?

Dashing from cover, a small, black cat rushed up toward Arynne before skidding to a halt a mere two feet from her. It stared at her with wide, green eyes. Flicking its long black tail, the two beings stared at each other for a long, breathless moment.

"Hello? Where did you come from?" Arynne asked. She hadn't seen a cat on the estate her entire time there. *But it isn't impossible,* she thought.

Just then, a dog barked, and the cat whirled toward the sound.

"A dog?" Arynne questioned, but the cat didn't give her an answer, taking off at a sprint to dive once more into the foliage, leaving the woman perplexed as to what had just happened.

There were no further sounds or appearances of strange animals for several minutes.

Hmm, must be pets of one of the invaders. She hadn't noticed anyone carrying animals the other night, but to be fair, that had been the least of her worries.

"Did you hear?" a voice echoed up from one of the left side paths, a woman's voice that Arynne didn't recognize. There were two other women chittering with her.

"Corrina is getting thrown out!" a second voice said before the first speaker could tell them.

"What happened?" asked the third voice.

"I don't know," the first one admitted. "I just saw her with Brutus and one of the new guys walking her to pack her things. They're sitting out front now, waiting for a ride. And she's crying her head off."

"If I'm honest, I'm not surprised. She kept throwing herself at him," said the third voice.

"I was wondering about that," the second voice said.

"Honestly, it's her own fault," stated the third voice. "You don't choose Dion. He chooses you."

"I think she thought she could reign over us all or something," snorted the second voice.

Their voices were already getting softer as they moved down the path as it curved away.

"What do you think the deal is with that pregnant housekeeper? She seems to have the same attitude."

"Yeah, well, Ecstasy is working on getting her out, too. Apparently, she has the same intentions."

"We don't know what her deal is, so just leave it to Ecstasy to solve."

"I'm sorry. It's just—" the voice huffed. "I'm really getting sick of this, you know? Everyone knows what the deal is. Dion belongs to all of us. I'm sick of all these ... these idiots trying to *possess* him."

"Like I said," the third voice stressed. "Let Ecstasy take care of it. She's the best at handling these situations. She'll keep him safe."

Finally, the voices drifted beyond intelligible.

So that was the way it was. That woman who had tried to be with Dion was kicked out, and Arynne was on the chopping block to be next.

"I *am* just a whore," she said, seeing their short time together for what it was. She had even received compensation with a job and a home, and now she was crossing the lines by wanting more. "I am such an idiot."

And for the first time in ages, Arynne wanted to go home.

"No, I can't," she said softly out loud, hoping that hearing those words would sway her own heart, but they didn't.

She thought of her father. Slipping the detective's card out, she stared down at the number. She had believed that if her father found her, it would be the worst thing in the world for her, but what exactly did she think he would do to her? If he meant to throw her out or disown her, then why try to find her at all? Anything else he would do to her... well, didn't she deserve it after what she had done, betraying her family? Her father was many things, many she could only imagine, but she was his daughter. And she carried his grandchild. Those things would matter to him as well.

"*What kind of life do you want?*" Dion's words came back to her, but she heard them with bitter ears this time. It was an easy thing for him to say when he could have anything he wanted in the world. She only had the pick of the least of bad choices.

Slowly, she lifted the phone she had waiting on her lap, sitting in the one spot where she got the best reception.

With her thumb, she dialed the number, then let out a breath before hitting send and ending her life here once and for all.

24

Dion breathed a sigh of relief when he spotted Arynne sitting, gazing over the lookout spot by the storage shed. He had been running all over the estate trying to find her. At some point while he had been gone, a new fence had been built, and she leaned against that while sitting on an old wooden folding chair. Her hair danced in the wind off the ocean, blowing gently, and when he called her name, she turned to look at him. Even in the full term of pregnancy, she looked so beautiful. A goddess of sensual desire.

"I am so sorry about this morning," he said before she could say anything. He crossed to her but aborted his intention to pull her into her arms when those dark eyes of hers continued to stare at him with no invitation, only cool blankness. It was the same imperious expression she had on her face when he had first met her, when he had been a stranger to her—one she hadn't decided to trust yet.

I have to fix this, he thought urgently.

He dropped down next to her, onto his knees so he was looking up at her.

"What do you want, sir?" she asked.

"I... sir?" The pounding in his head had not improved as the day had worn on. He stretched a hand to lay over hers, but she pulled away. "I'm sorry," he repeated, lifting his hands away and holding them up to show he meant no harm.

"You should be asleep," Arynne said, turning her head to look back out at the water. "You look like hell."

"Corinna is leaving," Dion said, ignoring her true statement and substituting it with one of his own.

"Because of me?" she asked flatly.

"Well, yes," he stated, then double-blinked at himself. "No, I mean... She shouldn't have done that anyway."

"Crawled into bed with you?"

"Try to take me like that!" he shouted and pressed a fist into his temple. "I didn't want it, and she kept forcing her way in. And I'm a goddam child who just can't say no, apparently." He dropped back off his knees onto his butt. "We have strict rules. No one forces anything on anyone ever, and she broke the rules, so she has to go."

He looked up at Arynne, pleading for understanding, and her eyes had softened at his tantrum.

Which wasn't what he wanted. He didn't want pity.

"I'm sorry. This..." He shook his head, but it didn't help clear it. He tried to crack his usual charming smile. "This isn't... I'm a mess."

"Like I said, you should go to bed."

"Not until I explain myself. I need you to understand."

Arynne sighed. "Look, I'd rather you not. You are causing enough trouble for me as it is."

"Trouble?" He furrowed his brow.

"With your other women," she stated.

"Who's said what to you?" he demanded, already seeing red. He imagined throwing them all out on their butts.

She worked her lips a second, hesitating.

"What did they say to you?" he pressed.

"They don't have to say anything," she said, then rubbed her hands over her large belly. "There is enough evidence for them to wonder, and like you said, your little group has rules, and I don't fit any of them."

"That shouldn't matter."

"Why?" she demanded. "Who am I to you?"

"You're..." he hesitated. He didn't have a name for this. He chose a word, but he knew it was inadequate for what she was. "You are my friend."

Her smile at that was sickly and bitter. "With benefits," she added.

"You came to me," he snapped.

"Yes, I violated the rules, too. I came to you. Hell, I threw myself at you like she did. Therefore, I need to leave as well."

He shook his head. "I don't want that. I said yes. I wanted you."

"I think sleeping with you was a mistake."

"Please, don't say that," Dion begged. But he knew it was true as soon as she said the words.

"No, it's okay. I don't blame you. Neither of us knew, but these are the consequences."

"Arynne, just stop a moment." He rubbed his head. "Dammit, I need a drink."

The hard look returned to her eye. "Is this the life you want, Dion?" she asked.

"What?"

"This. All this." She gestured at all of him.

"Yes!" he shouted, finally getting angry. "Yes, this is my life, Arynne. This is what I want!"

And I want you in it! but he didn't say that out loud. Those words were caught in the maelstrom in his head. He stood up then, filled with a need to get away. As desperate as he had been to find her and explain, he was more desperate now to escape.

She stood then. "Good!" she shouted after him. "Then I made the right decision!"

He stopped and spun back toward her, his anger fueling him. "What decision?"

Her hand went to the small of her back with a wince, and he spurted forward to help her, but she straightened before he got two steps. Black eyes glared at him with fire as she moved to push past him down the path.

"Arynne! What decision?"

"I'm going home!" she snapped.

Just then, the world began to spin. Dust whirled up around them, and they were lost in an impromptu cyclone. Overhead, a black helicopter crested over the ridge, making the trees around them dance violently. It continued to hover, and Dion moved to stand between Arynne and the pair of glass eyes with two humans as pupils. He tried to shield her from the wind that had turned her hair into a tangled mess. She didn't remain in the shelter of him though, but instead moved away, going down the path toward the house.

Once she had moved on, the helicopter lifted up more and redirected itself higher to hover over the estate.

Dion spent too long gawking at it and lost track of Arynne by the time he turned around. Panic overtook him, and he started running down one of the many branching paths that went toward the house. Or at least he thought he had, but he didn't know his way as well as he thought and got turned around.

Meanwhile, up in the sky, the helicopter hovered awhile, then lowered itself to the front of the main house.

"Dammit!" he cursed and decided to make his own path through foliage. The vines and prickly bushes held him back and scratched his skin, but he kept pushing until he broke through onto a more familiar path.

Several of the bacchanalia were gathered at the back terrace, peering in through the large windows and talking to each other as they spied.

"What's happening?" he gasped at them.

They all gaped at his sudden appearance, but he didn't care. He pressed himself against the window to peer into the darker interior compared to the bright light of the outside.

He just made out the back of Eileen and Zephyr as they stood on either side of Arynne by the door. There were two bags at their feet.

"No," he said urgently and pushed his way through the women, who all flashed him worried and confused looks. Grabbing the terrace door, he struggled to turn the tiny handle, and it slipped through his hands twice before he finally wrenched the door open.

By then, another pair of figures had entered the main room.

The sight of the two figures jarred him.

"Sorry, boss," Brutus said as he stepped in front of Dion, just as he moved to cross the room. The larger man held a hand out before himself, blocking Dion with no uncertain determination.

"Get out of my way," Dion hissed.

"She asked me to keep you back," Brutus stated, making it clear he answered to a higher authority.

"Ecstasy is not your boss!" he growled out.

"It wasn't Ecstasy that asked me," Brutus replied.

Just over Brutus's shoulder, Dion could see the older man go over to Arynne. She took a small step back, but then when he opened his arms, she went into them. Zephyr picked up her bags and moved past them toward the door.

"I can't—" Dion tried to argue, but Brutus set a hand on his shoulder and shook it.

"It's the rules, boss. She's made her choice. You got to let her go," Brutus stressed.

"I can stop it. I can fix it," Dion said too loudly, his voice echoing in the space. Eileen glanced over her shoulder back at him. She shook her head.

"Come on," Brutus insisted, putting his other hand against Dion's chest and pushing him backward out the still open terrace door.

"No! You can't—" But even if he had been in a better place to fight back, he hadn't been prepared for the larger man to strong-arm him out.

Arynne slipped the headphones over her head as she settled into the helicopter's seat. One of the men inside assisted her in putting the straps on around her belly. "We won't be up for very long," he assured her over the headphones. Arynne didn't care. She just wanted to get out of there.

"Put your legs together. He's not going to fuck a fat cow like you, so try to act like a lady," her father said crassly as he settled in next to her. She hadn't expected the direct insult so quickly after his performance of the worried, loving father inside for the entire compound watching, but Arynne said nothing and tried to do as her father ordered. Her belly and the difficulty balancing made the task nearly impossible, but that was fine. This was what she deserved, after all. At least she was going back to where she belonged.

25

"That was the last of them," Ecstasy cried out with relief as she came back through the front door, slamming it fantastically behind her. Dion didn't react as he continued to stare out the large window. He wore nothing but a pair of loose-fitting pants as he slouched low in one of the armchairs that usually sat in a cluster to the left of the room. He had dragged it over to the central window, so he could stare straight out of it, his back to the chaos as it had unfolded behind him.

Now there was quiet, the main room of the large house echoing like a tomb.

It was almost over.

Ecstasy came up beside him but went straight to the dining table where several rows of liquor, basically everything that had been brought with the bacchanalia, sat lined up three rows deep. She selected an expensive bourbon, uncorked the top and shotgunned a good two fingers of it directly from the bottle before she came up for air.

"A 'thank you' would be nice," she stated, staring daggers at him.

Dion didn't respond to it.

"Trying to book a dozen plane tickets to different places across the world, never mind severance packages for those that actually worked for us, and then soothing all those wounded feelings. That was absolute hell, but you know, you know, you're welcome."

Still, he said nothing. He didn't even look at her.

"You know what? It's fine," Ecstasy concluded for herself when it was clear that he wasn't going to respond. She heaved a big dramatic sigh and took another swig from the bottle. "We needed to start fresh anyway. We'll hire a whole new staff and develop a new show entirely. The old one was getting stale, and I'm not the only one who thought so. You can take this opportunity to get your butt back into the recording studio and get focused on the new album, and I'll start interviewing for—"

"You're fired, Ecstasy."

For a breath, he thought she was just going to keep talking as if she hadn't heard him, but then the words dropped off into a furious silence.

"What?" she asked with an edge that could cut glass.

To be fair, he had surprised himself when he had said the words out loud. Now that he had, he sat up, rubbing his hands on the velvety arms of the chair. With deliberate slowness, he dragged his gaze up at her. Her nostrils flared as her eyes went maddeningly wide. He couldn't hold her gaze for long, so he leaned his elbows on his knees and returned to looking at the pool outside.

"I can't go on like this, X. It's all too much," he stated.

Ecstasy let out a long, slow breath. "Okay, okay. I hear you, D," she said, bottling her rage back up behind her cool, professional, relatable self. Just another sign that she wasn't really hearing him at all.

She continued, "It's been a non-stop couple of years. Heck, I'll admit that even I am a little burned out, okay? Just... just let me pull a few strings. You need to take a break. I recognize that. Yeah. You're going to take a break. Maybe a month vacation? Get rested up, get some massages and yoga, and you know, take in the scenery. I can even get you some very welcoming housekeepers, whatever you want. But..."

She took a few steps back into his vision, pulling his attention back to her serious face. "But then we got to knuckle down and get to work, you understand?"

He wished he could feel angry. Feel something. Anything that would make what he knew he had to do easier. "You just don't understand, X. It's over," he said out loud, as much to himself as to her.

"What the living fuck do you mean it is over!?" she screamed, spitting the words in his face. "Nothing is over!"

"Yes, it is. I'm sorry—"

"Cut the damn bullshit, you're sorry. How dare you? How dare you after everything I have done for you. You think you can fire *me*? Me of all people. I own you, son. I own this brand, this *brand*, the cushy lifestyle you've been enjoying for the past decade? It all belongs to me. Without me, you would still be that skinny, sixteen-year old kid from bumfuck Minnesota!"

Some part of him heard the absurdity of that statement. A voice that wasn't his own, a more feminine, maternal voice said, "That's not how linear time works." He could almost smile at that statement.

"Shut the fuck up! Just shut up! You don't get to talk here. Do you understand how much trouble you will be in if I wasn't here to help you? You've got contracts, Dion! You signed your name to things for a shit ton of money, a lot of which you have already spent, and if we don't keep producing what we promised, all of it goes away. You'll be left with nothing, and they will sue you into oblivion. And whatever the fuck you do have left, believe me, I will take from you. I will make it my life's mission to make sure that Dionysus is wiped off the face of the earth. You think your dear old daddy will help you out? Not a fucking chance!"

He knew everything she was saying was probably true. But there was nothing in him that cared anymore. "You don't understand. It's over," he said.

"Fuck you! Fuck you! Fuck you!" she shouted and kept saying as she flung the remains of the bourbon bottle onto the floor at his feet. It broke but not in the way she intended. Part of the neck snapped, but otherwise the bottle just spun in place, spewing alcohol over his bare feet.

She continued to swear at him, but he didn't respond. Just sat there and took it all. This was a hell of his own making, and he knew it. It was his to endure.

"Okay, that's enough," another voice said after Ecstasy's voice rang off the walls for several minutes.

The interruption made both him and Ecstasy turn toward the door, but Zephyr was already crossing the room.

"What the fuck do you want, Twink?" she shot at him as he placed himself between her and Dion.

"Look, if you're going to insult me, pick something that makes sense. Now get your skinny ass out of here. You've done enough."

"You can't—" she started to say, but then her eyes drifted back toward the door, and her eyes went wide as someone else approached from that direction. She took a step back, clearly intimidated.

A second man approached, one that had changed so much, it took Dion a long moment to recognize him. When he stopped next to Zephyr, he leaned forward toward Ecstasy.

"Hello, Andrea," Erik said softly. If there was anyone that actually intimidated Ecstasy, it was Erik Pandemos. Dion had no idea why, neither of them had ever said, but it worked on his former manager. She took a sexually defiant posture before moving a couple steps forward to wrap her arms around Erik's neck.

"Why Erik, it's so wonderful to see you again—" She leaned in for a kiss, only to have Erik grab her face in one hand. Immediately, her sexy façade disintegrated.

"No," he whispered to her.

She took another step back, and Zephyr stepped up beside Erik.

"You're going to leave now," Zephyr said.

Looking between the two of them, her face twisted into an ugly mask of rage and fear.

Finally, she landed that hateful gaze on Dion in the gap between his two friends, crossing her arms defiantly. "You'll be hearing from my lawyer," she informed him and then turned on her heel to march out.

Erik and Zephyr exchanged a glance, and Zephyr followed Ecstasy out, probably to make sure she went. Dion didn't care; he just felt relief the second she went out the door.

"She doesn't have her bags," Dion said, realizing she had left empty-handed, which meant she could come back.

"Zephyr will make sure she has everything that is hers," Erik countered, coming around the chair to look out the main view, giving Dion time to take his old friend's new look in. Physically, he looked much the same, lithe with his dark hair and blue eyes, though the hair was cut shorter now from when Dion had last seen him. He also wore color now, his usual dark clothing replaced with a light blue Hawaiian shirt with purple flowers dotting it over a pair of light-colored pants.

"I never wanted to see you again," Dion stated.

"Yeah, well, that was the old Erik. He's dead now," Erik said, grinning as he quoted their favorite show.

"You look happy," Dion said, realizing it was true.

"You look like shit," Erik countered. "And yes. I am happy."

Dion shook his head. "I don't even remember what that feels like," he said.

"When's the last time you had a shower?" Erik asked.

The former superstar rock god could only shrug and hang his head. "Dammit, I'm pathetic."

"We all break eventually."

Zephyr rejoined them, adding a cuff to the back of Dion's head for good measure. "She's gone. You're welcome."

"I'm sorry, Zephyr," Dion tried to say as he rubbed his head, but his friend waved it away.

"Save it for someone who deserves it," he said as he pulled out a chair from the table.

"I thought you left with Eileen?" Dion asked, sitting up to reach over for the abandoned bourbon bottle, but Erik got to it first and walked it over toward the kitchen instead.

Zephyr stared at him. "No, Eileen went with Arynne."

That made Dion start in his chair. "What?"

"You didn't notice? You were there when they left."

"I was..." Dion shook his head and pressed the heels of his hands into his eye sockets. "All I saw was her. I'm glad though. Arynne isn't alone."

"You are really in love with this woman, aren't you?" Erik said, returning from the kitchen holding a low-ball glass with some of the bourbon from the bottle draining through a small strainer. When the last of it passed through, he lifted the strainer out and gave it a little tap. He took a sip from the drink before he held it out.

Both men reached out for the glass, but Zephyr smacked Dion's hand to take it for himself. "Not for you. You need to dry out. Answer the man's question." Zephyr eyed the drink for glass shards but took a drink when he didn't find any.

"I don't have an answer," Dion said sullenly.

Zephyr threw up his hands as if saying, "See I told you," but Erik held his own out palm down, telling Zephyr to "Calm down. Give it a minute." On Erik's wrist, a gold chain glinted in the dull gray light. Dion focused on that chain, not surprised to see it. Erik was into that sort of symbolic bondage sort of thing, but the chain continued across the back of his hand and seemed to be connected to a ring on his finger. On the ring finger of his left hand.

"You're married?" he exclaimed, though it had as much energy as suffocating fish. He looked to Zephyr. "Did you know this?"

Zephyr crooked an eyebrow at him. "You sent them a present."

"Ten bucks Andrea is the one who sent the present," Erik said, still referring to Ecstasy by her given name.

"No bet."

Dion groaned. "What's wrong with me, Erik?"

"The things you wanted when you were sixteen are no longer serving you," he said simply.

Dion went still at that, like a bell had rung in his head. It was something he had almost thought himself but hadn't been able to form into complete words. He leaned forward again, holding his head as if to keep this new overwhelming revelation from escaping. "This is about my mother."

"These things always seems to always come back to that," Erik agreed.

"Well, I have a great relationship with my mother, so I don't know what your guys' problems are," Zephyr snarked.

"Your mother is your grandmother," Erik noted.

"I stand by my statement," Zephyr insisted, crossing his arms.

Dion ignored the banter; his mind was buzzing as pieces fell into place. A child's wish to please his dying mother's wish: that he pursue what would make him happy. And a child's misunderstanding that that goal could and in fact would change over time. What *did* he really want now? He wanted to say Arynne, but that wasn't quite right. He was going to keep thinking on it but now...

"I don't deserve Arynne. Not after all this," he said plainly. Letting himself hear it. "I abandoned her, and while I didn't cheat on her exactly, I..."

"She wanted you to be faithful?" Erik asked.

"*I* wanted to be faithful. I only wanted her. I just didn't..." Dion gestured with his head. "I just didn't put it together that that was why everything I normally did just felt awful. Like I was forcing myself to do it, not because I wanted to. And now it's too late."

"To convince her to be in a relationship with you? Yeah probably," Erik said. "For you to take the lesson and get on with recalibrating your life? Not at all."

Dion looked to his friends who met his gaze with the calm strength of two men who had gone through hell and come to pull him out of his.

"I am a lucky bastard, aren't I?" he said softly.

"The luckiest," Zephyr agreed.

"I'm going to go take a shower," Dion said. "Then let's get the fuck out of here."

"Dion," Zephyr interceded, "what do you want to do about Ecstasy? I mean, am I the only one here who thinks she's going to sue you?"

Dion regarded Zephyr a moment. "I have two choices to make in life..."

"Worrying about what other people are going to do or get on with living your life," Erik finished.

They regarded each other, nodding at the understanding. "Thank you for coming back, Erik," Dion said, clapping his lost friend on the shoulder.

Erik stopped him from moving on. "You were right," he said seriously. "You were right, and I was wrong."

Dion cracked a smile. "Yeah, I know."

They nodded, letting the issue between them lay buried and forgotten.

"Okay, hurry up," Erik dismissed. "You look like a man no woman would touch."

26

"And you slept with him?" her father asked as he tucked another slice of roast beef into his mouth, chewing as he spoke casually, as if this was a normal subject for a father and a daughter to speak of.

Arynne sat there mortified, wishing she was anywhere else. Instead, she clenched her fingers so tightly they were white. "Yes, father," she said.

Her father, Cesare, didn't look at her or react, just stared off while he chewed. "And you're sure the baby isn't his?" he asked.

"No, it is not," she said, forcing her words to be civil.

"Hmm. Pity. He is easier to get to than Thomas." Her father sat back, lifting his glass of wine to his lips while he continued to think.

"Thomas..." Arynne's grip tightened on her spoon, staring at the simple soup she was eating. Her stomach had been sour since coming home. It was getting worse now. "Has there been any word from Thomas?"

Now her father looked at her, his eyes full of the accusations he hadn't voiced yet since bringing her back home. There was no mistaking that Arynne was his daughter, at least as far as looks were concerned. He had a fit figure for a man his age, and where his black hair had turned bright silver, it was cut in an up-to-date style. One could call him stylish if it wasn't for his petulant behavior.

Arynne fingered her water glass, hating herself that she was still unable to meet those eyes. Instead, she focused on the two pre-natal vitamins that had been presented with dinner on their own little dish. The clothing she wore was pregnancy stylish, designed by some big name in Paris. Her father had even returned the jewels she owned. The diamond tennis bracelet on her wrist glittered in the late afternoon sun. Staring at it now, she wondered why she hadn't taken it with her when she ran away with Thomas. While they could have used it, she also knew she hadn't wanted to take anything to do with her father.

They were supposed to start over.

And here she was, right back where she had been before.

Except that I chose this this time, she thought.

"No," her father finally said. "I've had people out searching high and low for him. It is like he disappeared, though I think I know what happened."

She dared to meet his gaze this time, genuinely wanting to know.

"Once he pried the secrets of the Labyrinth program out of you, we had a security breach in our mainframe. The damage is irreversible. The server is ransom locked, but we've gotten no ransom notice. The Minotaur is dead."

Arynne knew it was. The programs she had designed to protect her father's vast financial empire had been laid open for Thomas by herself. Both the legal and illegal ones.

"I'll never be able to set foot in America again," her father grumbled as if that were the most of his worries. There was no extradition treaty with his island, and he had plenty of other countries protecting him.

"But if Thomas hasn't ransomed the system, why would—"

"We will not speak of this!" her father shouted, slamming his hand on the tabletop, making the silverware and glassware jump. Arynne held still, wondering if her father's hand would fly at her, but instead, Cesare mastered himself. "As long as I live, you will never have anything to do with my business again. Your only job now will be to marry decently enough and give me legitimate grandchildren that have more sense than you."

He threw his napkin onto his plate and shoved it away, his appetite lost.

"I'm sorry, Father," she repeated softly, near tears.

"I tried to be one of those modern fathers, and what did it get me? You have a brilliant mind for numbers and languages, and it all went straight out the window the minute some pretty boy diddles you! Worthless. Absolutely worthless! Now all that is left is to get you married off and in such a way that I may be able to recover from all of this mess."

She caught what he said the second time. "You want me to get married?"

"It was always the plan for you, child," he said, downing the last of his wine and thrusting the glass out to a waiting footman to refill it.

"And who am I supposed to marry?" she asked evenly, trying not to give away any feelings she would otherwise have. It was just her father and her at the table, but she could feel all the eyes of his security hovering around the edges of his garden terrace. They were more overt than any other time she could remember, but she wasn't sure if it was because of her or a result of what she had done.

Her father leaned back and sighed, rubbing the bridge of his nose. "I have a few ideas. The pool is smaller now than before, but there are a handful of those who would still take you, especially if you can get the baby weight off. Actually, if you can get the weight off, that will open a few things up again for you. Maybe could get an old husband that will leave you everything in a few years. Give you some options. You're lucky *being* my daughter. That in itself gives you some value. I have taken a significant blow, but I am by no means de-throned. Just don't embarrass me anymore."

A heavy pause laid over them. Arynne knew she was supposed to feel guilty, but she didn't. But her father couldn't be allowed to know that. "I'm sorry, Father."

He didn't acknowledge her continued apology, but he did hear it, sneaking his fingers back under his plate to snag another bite of his half-eaten roast. "Well, the first thing we are going to do to solve this mess is you are going to claim that Dionysus, or Dion whatever, *is* the father of your child."

Arynne's eyes went wide as the spoon slipped from her fingers to drop onto the ground. "What?" The footman scurried forward to collect it, then disappeared, possibly to fetch her another one.

"It will be an easy thing. We won't even have to prove anything with a paternity test. We'll offer to settle for a tidy amount, and he'll take it just to make the problem go away."

"Father, please, don't do this. He was nothing but kind to me—"

"Oh, shut up. He took advantage of you and the situation, and you're the idiot who fell for it. Twice!" Cesare snapped at the nearby footman, who wasn't there, still off getting her a clean spoon. Cesare turned in his seat looking for him as he continued talking. “I’ve had the lawyer contact him. It’s already done. I probably shouldn’t have even told you. Old habits that I’m going to have to correct. Since it’s now proved I can’t trust you.”

She couldn’t say anything. She knew there was no point, but it sank her misery even more. Ecstasy had been right; she should have signed something declaring Dion wasn’t the father of her baby. Dion just never brought it up again later, and Arynne knew she would never do something like that to hurt him. She should have never come home.

“You know, I’m getting the impression that you are not grateful for everything I’ve done for you,” her father declared, the footman finally returning to present her with a clean spoon. Her father snatched it from her hand. “After everything you did. Everything I’ve had to do to recover from what you did.”

“I am, Father,” Arynne protested gently.

“Because you’re just sitting there sulking while I’m bending over backwards to fix everything for you and your bastard.” He threw down his napkin in disgust and leaned back to cross his legs.

“I’m very grateful, Father. I’m just so tired,” she admitted. It was true. The last few weeks of this pregnancy was doing her in. Her feet and ankles had swollen, making it even harder to walk, and if it wasn’t for the cushion in her lower back, it would have been more difficult for her to sit as long as she had.

Before her father could launch into another string of hurtful, burdensome words, her father’s butler arrived on the terrace.

“Excuse me, sir. There is a Mr. Brewer here to see you. He says you invited him.”

Arynne's heart dropped into her stomach. Involuntarily, she stood from her seat, which was quite a feat, considering she needed to grip the table as she wobbled.

"Who?" her father demanded, disgusted at the interruption.

"Dion," Arynne breathed, unable, and unwilling, to hold back her excitement. "He's here?"

The butler looked down his nose at her but nodded stiffly. "Yes, I believe so," he said, then returned his attention to her father. "He says he wishes to speak to you about your..." The butler cleared his throat none-too subtly. "Paternity suit against him."

Arynne's heart sank, though she wondered what she had expected. Now she wanted to run or waddle to her room and hide, but no. She owed it to him to look him in the eye as he saw what a disgrace she truly was. She needed to face him.

Her father stood up, clearing his throat uncomfortably. "Alright then. I assume he has his lawyer with him?"

The butler shook his head. "No, sir. He came alone."

"Oh." Now that took her father aback. He turned to Arynne. "Is he a really savvy sort or is he just a confident idiot?"

"He's..." Arynne had no idea what to say. "He's a good man," she settled on.

"Idiot then. Alright, well, tell him I'll meet him in my office." Her father turned to go, gesturing toward the footman. "When she's done, take her to room and call the midwife to check up on her. She should have had this bastard any damn day by now."

The footman bowed his head in acknowledgment, but Arynne moved around the table. "Father, please. Let me see him."

The way her father turned to her, she thought he would say no, but something passed behind his calculating eyes. "As you wish," he said with his more familiar gallantry, the old-world gentleman he liked to play, that she had always thought he was when she was a child.

Yet when she had been a child, he would have offered her his arm to lead her into the next room. Instead, he grabbed up his wine glass and walked off into the house too quickly for her to follow easily. She knew he was being deliberately cruel.

When she just couldn't make it, she paused in one of the halls leading toward his office. Chairs were set up there, not for her benefit but because it was how the place had been styled. Heaving a heavy breath, she settled on one, the pain in her lower back growing insistent for a moment. Blowing out a breath, she rubbed her fingers in as best she could, trying to get the muscle to release, but it just didn't seem to be working. That particular spot in her back had been charley horsing all morning, every time she had moved too fast. After a few moments, it did pass.

Just when she had gathered herself to get back up on her feet to continue on, she heard *his* voice echoing down the hall.

Suddenly, she couldn't do it. She couldn't face him, not after everything. Urgently, she turned toward the T-junction of the hall and went back out the short distance to the rear garden. She had no idea where she thought she would go. Just away.

On this side of the house, the terrace cascaded down the side of the hill the house was built on with a string of pools that echoed the same, pouring one into another. Its other blessed virtue was that the walkway and stairs here had a railing on one side that she could lean on. About halfway down near a copse of trees and a branching path through them, her lower back seized again, sharp and painful.

"Dammit," she hissed through her teeth and leaned against the rail to try to relieve it. "I am so done with being pregnant!"

"Arynne!"

His voice was so close. She gasped as she whirled around. Dion stopped a few feet away when she turned, his eyes wide with concern, his hand caught in mid-air extended out to her. He looked so handsome in his three-piece suit, his hair back into a tight ponytail at the back of his neck, but that wasn't what made him look so wonderful to her. He had always been handsome, but the attraction went deeper in spite of his appearance. It was like the gripping hand on her heart finally tore away to reach for him, and everything she had thought since leaving the island estate came roaring in, finally able to scream free.

"What took you so long?" she asked, her voice cracking.

Chapter 27

He crossed then, throwing his arms around her, and she moved toward him with what speed she could to grip him back just as hard around his waist. He pressed his cheek against the top of her head and rocked her back and forth, even if it was awkward to do around her belly. "I'm here. I'm here."

"I love you," she said, the only truth that mattered in that moment.

"I love you, too," he replied, but as much as she wanted to, she didn't believe it.

"No, no. Don't just say that because I did," she said, pushing herself up so she could look into his face, but he kissed her as soon as she lifted her eyes. It was a chaste kiss, just their lips, yet with such force and fire behind it, it was like he was breathing her heart back to life.

Another pain gripped her back, this never-ending charley horse threatening to snap her spine in two. She hissed through her teeth, breaking the kiss sooner than she wanted to.

"Arynne!" Dion cried urgently, but she held up a hand to press calm into his chest.

"It's nothing. It's nothing. You just bent me too far back, and my lower back is cramping," she said. "It's been happening all week."

"Do you want to sit down?" he asked, scanning for somewhere to do that.

"There's a bench," she indicated through the small dirt path that branched off into the copse of trees, a tiny oasis where one could sit and listen to songbirds. They were gossiping like mad at that time of day, unperturbed by whatever the humans were doing below them. With a hand on her back, he took her other hand to guide her off the path, and she let him. She savored the feeling of his arm around her and wished it was all that she would think about.

But it wasn't.

"I didn't know," she said, knowing no other way to start but to dive in. "About the paternity suit. I just found out."

"It's alright," Dion said, dismissing it as if it was nothing, but it wasn't.

"No, it's not alright!" Arynne insisted. "Don't do that! Don't just ... take everything in stride like that. This is important!"

Gods, she felt so tired. They made it to the bench, a small wooden thing, sturdy but more or less forgotten with its paint peeling in places. What she really wanted was to lay down. Her feet throbbed, and it was getting harder and harder to breathe.

"You're right. I'm sorry," Dion capitulated, standing in front of her to watch as she leaned forward to breathe.

"Are you sure you're alright?" he asked.

"It just hurts like a son of a bitch," she said, the swearing definitely helping as the pain in her back eased. "Believe me—I've been told that if it was 'go time' it would hurt a lot more and all over. This is just a muscle cramp from trying to move too fast."

Dion did not look wholly mollified, but he yielded as he glanced at his watch. "I'm supposed to be meeting with your father now," he said.

"Like I said, I'm sorry," Arynne said, her heart heavy. "You didn't have to come."

"I wanted... I needed to see you," he said.

"Because you love me," she said. Why was that revelation not a good thing? Why didn't it make her heart sing? She could leave there, escape her father's house, and start the life she actually wanted with this man.

Because it was the same thing all over again. It solved nothing, resolved nothing. She didn't want to be another one of his harem. She was jealous of the other women in his life, and she chided herself for how wrong that felt.

"I don't want to own you, Dion," she said. "But I do, and I know that's not what you want or nee—"

The pain lanced into her back again, cutting her words off, and she leaned forward. This time she closed her eyes against it, forgetting to breathe through.

"Arynne, I think you're in labor," Dion said carefully.

"NO!" she denied. "That can't be what's happening. My water hasn't even broken."

Fate laughed at her at that moment as something tickled down her legs. Urgently and with no care for decorum or propriety, Arynne pulled up the side of her skirt and brushed her hand along her inner thigh. The insides of her legs were warm.

"When... when did this happen?" she asked staring at the pink-tinged fluid.

"Okay, we can shelve all other talk. We need to get you to the house."

He tried to lift her up to her feet, but she buckled nearly immediately.

"Oh, I don't think I can!" she called out.

She went to the ground, onto all fours as Dion guided her down, only able to keep her from landing too hard. Being on all fours helped, shifting the pain she felt from her back to all throughout her stomach.

"Oh gods! The baby is coming!" she cried out. She rolled herself onto her back and screamed. There was no time! It couldn't be here!

"Dion!" she sobbed out, and he grabbed the hand she stretched out to him. "I don't want to have my baby in the dirt!"

"It'll be okay. I'm here," he said, being so infuriatingly calm about the whole thing.

He slipped off his suit jacket then, laying it down on the ground, snug right up against her.

"What are you doing?!" she exclaimed, but it was too late to do or say anything more. This time instead of screaming, she bore down. Gods, it felt so good to bear down! Everything lined up like it was supposed to, and something passed hard between her legs.

"You got this; you got this, Arynne!" Dion called. She had no idea what he was doing, her skirt was caught at her knees, creating a screen so she couldn't see. Time seemed to be warping all around her. How long had she been out here?

He had knelt down between her legs, and while his voice remained calmed, his eyebrows were scrunched together with worry. "What's happening?"

"It's fine. You're doing fine," he said, meeting her eyes.

"Don't fucking lie to me, Dion Brewer!" she growled, but then the shudder spasmed through her again, and she bore down. This time pushing gave immediate relief and pleasure as the baby passed from her body.

A second later, a baby screamed its voice to the world for the first time. Dion pushed back her skirt and lifted a small, slimy creature up onto her stomach, warm and pink and squirming.

"She's here, Arynne!" Dion shouted, so excited.

Arynne stared down at the little creature laying against her. It chirped another cry, then gave a big sigh, like it had found that whole ordeal exhausting and was glad it was over. Carefully, Arynne laid her hands on the little body, and miracle of miracles, the baby lifted her head to look up at her with beautiful crystal blue eyes. She chirped again, then laid her head back down.

"Dia," Arynne breathed.

"What?" Dion asked. He was beside her now, keeping another hand on the baby's back as he leaned in to hear what she said.

Arynne looked up at him, glad that it was his face she saw in that moment. Never wanting to look away from that face. "Her name is Dia," she said, the female version of Dion.

His face crumpled then, tears beading out of his own eyes as his face screwed up into an ugly pucker. She felt serenely happy and touched his cheek with her free hand. He pressed it in and cried some more before sliding down to kiss the top of Dia's head, heedless of any grossness she might have on her.

Then he was stripping off his vest and shirt, so he could use the shirt to bundle the baby up to keep her warm despite the warmth of the day.

"What the hell is going on here?!" a rough voice shouted, and suddenly there were people all around. While most of them were men, Arynne couldn't follow the chaos much further. She felt so exhausted, and slowly she laid back her head and closed her eyes, holding her baby against her chest. Someone else could deal with this problem now.

It was a mere hour later, and Arynne lay in a clean bed, having gotten a shower with Eileen's help. She never let her baby out of her sight, even as her father's security guards carried her back up to the house. Dion had ahold of Dia the entire time once Eileen showed up to take care of the afterbirth and let him cut the cord.

None of the security guards argued with it.

Arynne didn't see a single hair of her father, and that was alright. She didn't care to.

Now she was back in bed. Someone had found Dion another shirt to wear, a plain black undershirt that was a size too big for him to be fashionable anymore. He didn't seem to care as he sat in an armchair next to her bed, holding little Dia, who had also been cleaned and bundled up from their ordeal.

"I can't believe I gave birth to her in the garden," Arynne said, shaking her head.

"Seven pounds, four ounces," Eileen declared proudly from the side table where she was writing things down in a file. "Not the most dramatic birth I attended. Ha—or didn't attend in this case."

"You were there for an important part. I had no idea what I was doing," Dion said.

"Really?" Arynne asked surprised. "You seemed so confident."

"Oh, I was dumping in my pants the whole time," Dion assured her.

"Charming," Arynne noted with faux disdain. Then they both laughed, their eyes warming on each other over their shared experience.

Eileen went over to Dion's side and gazed down at the baby in his arms. "She's beautiful," the midwife said, gently caressing the side of the sleeping baby's head.

The door to Arynne's room opened then, without knocking or ceremony, and Cesare strode in. He stared down at Dia in alarm, as if he had no idea there would be the baby in here. Arynne pushed herself up in the bed, and Dion stood with Dia still protectively in his arms.

"What the hell happened here?" Cesare demanded.

"I had a baby, Father," Arynne stated angrily.

"And what is he doing here?!" her father shouted, jerking a thumb at Dion.

"He was there when it happened," was all Arynne could say since it was the truth.

"Would you like to hold your granddaughter, sir?" Eileen said, setting a hand on Dion's shoulder, prepared to walk him over to Cesare with the baby if she had to.

"No, that's fine," Cesare said, again mastering himself. "Give the bastard to the midwife, Brewer. We'll talk in the other room."

"The what now?" Dion's hackles went up.

A grinning sneer took over Cesare's face. "*Your* bastard," the older man spat back, his eyes glittering with delight as he threw the lie at the younger man. "How could you take advantage of a vulnerable young woman who had been so cruelly abandoned like that? It's absolutely heartless."

"Father, please don't!" Arynne tried to insist, but her father never even looked her way.

"Are you going to take responsibility for your *bastard*? Oh, I suppose it makes sense. You are a *bastard* yourself."

Arynne had never seen rage on Dion before. His kind, smiling face had always been his default no matter how he was really feeling inside, but now his eyes snapped like lightning. Arynne thought her father would take a step back, but instead, he shifted his shoulders as if he were preparing, even daring, for Dion to punch him.

Then Dion turned his intensity toward Arynne. "I am Dia's father," he said to her.

She was gobsmacked. But she also understood what he was saying. "Really?" she asked, the voice of her heart sound small and hopeful.

"If you want me," he returned. "And only me."

Her head was nodding before she could speak. "Yes, yes, I want you."

"Wait," her father said, unable to understand what was happening, but neither of them cared.

Eileen brought over the file she had been working on, holding out the pen to Dion. With one hand still wrapped around his daughter, Dion took the pen and signed his name on her birth certificate, under father of the child. "Mine by love and law," he whispered, then crossed to Arynne to offer himself to her. She took his head and kissed him gently on the lips, sealing their promise.

"No, no, you're going to pay..." Cesare declared, snatching up the birth certificate from Eileen and waving it in Dion's face. Eileen snatched it back, annoyed, but undeterred from the grandfather's antics. She took it over to Arynne to sign.

"I'll be taking my fiancée and child home," Dion said, keeping his back to the man as if he wasn't a threat.

"Fiancée?" Cesare blinked. "What are you talking about?"

Arynne finished signing her name, then held her arms out for her daughter. Dion passed her over as Eileen went to the side table and began snapping pictures of the documents within.

"No, no you can't..." Cesare said, crossing too late to grab the forms, tearing them up in his hands.

"It's too late," Eileen said, her phone making a swishing sound. "I've already sent in the digital copies to be registered."

Her father whirled on Arynne, jabbing a finger toward her face. "You are dead to me. You hear me? Dead! I want you all out of my house, now!"

To everyone's relief, he stormed out.

"Can I leave?" Arynne asked, alarmed at being thrown out after barely having just given birth.

"Don't worry, child. I've done this battle before," Eileen said, pushing up her sleeves with the determination of a general. She exited the room, leaving Arynne and Dion alone with their child.

Arynne leaned back, exhausted. "Honestly, I can't wait to get out of this place. This was a huge mistake. But it'll be alright now, right? We'll go back to the island house."

"Arynne, there is something I need to tell you," Dion said, sitting on the edge of the bed. "First... I want you to know that these are extraordinary circumstances and pressures. You are not obligated to marry me if you decide later that you don't want to."

"Dion," she replied, setting a hand on his closest forearm. "I want to marry you."

"Well, you might not once you know..." He cleared his throat. "I'm probably going to lose everything. I walked away from a lot of obligations, and I'm probably going to have to file bankruptcy and stuff. There are several lawsuits, including one from Ecstasy—"

"Ecstasy?" she exclaimed, surprised.

He gave her a side-eye. "We don't agree on what the best course of action for my life is anymore."

"I see," was all she could say to that.

"It means all I have to offer you is a house in Minnesota. At least for now, until I get things sorted. Zephyr is helping me. And a couple of other friends. I don't know. Maybe it will all work out. It always seems to with me. But I want you to know that I didn't come here to pressure you into coming back with me. This isn't your problem, and I wouldn't blame you if you would rather walk away from this. I just had to come to make sure you were alright."

"So, they're all gone?" Arynne asked. "The Bacchanalia? You got rid of them."

Dion nodded his head. "I don't want all the women I *could* want anymore. I haven't for a while, but I was an idiot who thought he couldn't change his mind. It took hitting rock bottom for me to figure that out, and I can understand if it's too late now for you to forgive me or believe that I just want one person to share my life with now. I just want you, my friend, but you don't have to. You're not obligated to."

He reached back and stroked Dia's head gently, the little baby sighing in her sleep. "I would like you to come with me, if you want."

"To Minnesota?" He waited, breath held as she seemed to mull his words over. "I'd... I'd like to go to college," she said softly.

"Oh?" he said, his eyebrows rising.

She nodded. "Yes. And I'll find a way to pay for it myself, so you don't—"

He had never felt lighter in his life. "We can make it work! Whatever you want to do with your life, we'll make it happen together!" he assured. "I mean it, I really want this."

"I want it, too, Dion. If you mean it."

"I really do!" he insisted. He would mean it, for every day that he had left in his life. He would mean it and make sure she never regretted it.

He smiled, lacing his fingers with hers. "Thank you," he whispered and pressed his lips to her precious digits. "Thank you."

Epilogue

Thomas sat back at the small café, taking in the view of Paris as people walked along the Seine in the mild fall afternoon. It had been a while since he had felt so lonely, had really stopped long enough to even feel lonely. On the table, his phone pinged, alerting him of a message. Flipping it over, he smiled at the alert, a text banner that simply said, "It is done."

That was it then. The board had just elected him the CEO of his father's company. An email chimed a moment later confirming it. He had everything he had wanted. Everything was coming up aces for him.

Satisfied, Thomas leaned back, but the smile on his face slipped as he gazed over the city. Something inside him was missing, was marring his victory, but he had no idea what it could be. Wasn't this everything that he wanted?

"May I join you?"

The voice shook him out of his reverie, and he looked up at the stranger standing next to his table.

"Excuse me?" Thomas asked, a bit disgusted by the forwardness of this individual.

"May I sit down?" the stranger repeated.

Thomas cast an eye over the man, well dressed in a fine leather jacket over stylish pants that emphasized things in the right places. There was something familiar about the man's face, and it took a second longer for Thomas to figure it out.

"Wait, I know you. You're that singer ... Dionysus!"

The stranger grinned and offered his hand. "Just Dion, but yes."

Thrilled at meeting the celebrity, Thomas stood up and shook his hand heartily, both laughing as he did so. "Yes, yes, please join me. Though I have no idea why you would want to."

"Oh, I've heard a lot about you from a mutual friend. I heard you were here in Paris, and I actually came out to meet you in person."

"Well, I'm flattered," Thomas said sincerely. "I love your songs, man. You are one of the best. Legend."

"Well, thank you," Dion said in return, taking the other seat at the table while he dropped a pair of expensive sunglasses onto the surface. "It's been quite a year. I won't lie."

"Yeah, yeah, I heard about the controversies. Complete bullshit, seriously," Thomas sympathized.

"It'll be alright. I got good people supporting me. The comeback concert is going to be better than ever," the rock god assured. "And I have my family supporting me."

"Oh?" Thomas asked, not really interested but not going to be impolite. "I didn't know you were married. I thought your life was wine, women, and song. Literally."

Dion laughed. "Sure, and you'd be surprised how boring that got after a while."

"Sounds like the dream to me," Thomas said, saluting him with what was left of the wine he was drinking. "Would you like a glass?" he belatedly offered.

"Yes," Dion agreed, reaching into his coat and pulling something out of the inner pocket. Thomas poured out the remains of his bottle into an empty water glass he snagged from the unoccupied table nearby. "So, you don't, I take it?"

"Don't what?" Thomas asked, holding out the glass.

"Have the whole wife and children thing."

"Gods, no," Thomas snickered. "Not yet any way. Maybe I'll pick up a supermodel or something along the way. You know."

"I suppose it's hard to look at any woman after you've let the best woman in the world get away," Dion said, taking a long drink of the offered wine.

Something about that question felt like a smack at the back of Thomas's head. "Excuse me?" he said, arresting his companionable laughter.

Dion's own joviality seemed to cool into a knowing smirk that hinted at danger.

"Arynne Minoa. Well, Brewer now," the superstar said. He held up the thing he had hidden in his pocket. It was a slightly battered envelope, which he opened, unfolding the trio-folded pieces of paper within, before setting them down before Thomas on the table.

Thomas shifted away from them as if a viper had been placed in front of him. "What the hell is that?"

"Paperwork renouncing any possible claim you could have on *my daughter*," Dion said as if it was the most natural thing in the world. "Being the one that contributed to her genetics and all."

"I... I don't have a daughter," Thomas said, unsure of the truth of that statement and so shocked that he didn't have time to convincingly lie.

"Dia," Dion said. "Her name is Dia. Like a diamond. You helped conceive her on the last night you saw Arynne, when you screwed her and then screwed her again by leaving."

"I don't have to listen to this," Thomas said, standing up urgently. He found his exit blocked by a wall made up of two men behind him.

"And if you sign this, you will never hear it again. I promise. I have claimed her as my own, but... well, let's just say this is covering all asses." Dion stood up and held out a pen toward Thomas. "Two seconds, no problems."

Thomas eyed the pen, then took it. An exact two seconds later, it was done.

Dion smiled, took the piece of paper back, and snapped a quick picture of it with his phone. "Thanks, guys," he said to the two burly men behind Thomas.

Both cracked into silly smiles. "Yeah, no problem. That was funny," said one in broken English while the other slapped his companion as he took the euros Dion offered them. They both walked off chortling.

Dion tucked the paper back into its envelope and returned it to the inner pocket of his jacket. "Thank you. That was much easier than I thought it would be."

"Wait, what just..." Thomas asked, so distracted he didn't see Dion's punch across his face until it had already hit. Thomas dropped to the ground at the other man's feet. He clutched at his eye, but before he could do much to retaliate, Dion pushed him with a foot and placed that foot on his chest. "And if you ever come near me or mine again," he warned, leaning closer so his soft words could be heard, "I will smite you from the earth. Do you hear me, little man?"

Thomas didn't respond, and the god above him didn't seem to need him to. He pressed hard once with his foot and turned to walk away as if this was nothing. Thomas scrambled back to his feet, spitting and cursing. Nobody who stood there staring said anything to him.

"What the hell are you all looking at?" he shouted at them.

"Sir, we will have to ask you to leave," a waiter with fairly good English said.

"I'm leaving. I'm leaving," Thomas said, straightening his jacket. "You'll never see me again."